Night Swimming

Night

Swimming

Aaron Starmer

Penguin Workshop

PENGUIN WORKSHOP
An imprint of Penguin Random House LLC
1745 Broadway, New York, New York 10019

First published in the United States of America by Penguin Workshop,
an imprint of Penguin Random House LLC, 2025

Visit us online at penguinrandomhouse.com.

Library of Congress Cataloging-in-Publication Data is available.

Printed in the United States of America

ISBN 9780525555643

1st Printing

LSCC

Design by Mary Claire Cruz

This is a work of historical fiction. Apart from the well-known actual people,
events, and locales that figure in the narrative, all names, characters, places,
and incidents are the products of the author's imagination or are used
fictitiously. Any resemblance to current events or locales, or to living persons, is
entirely coincidental.

For Hannah and Rowan, who refuse
to stop growing up—AS

As I watch you sleep, I sing to myself, soft and mournful, a calming melody that laps against the shores of my addled mind. I doubt you can hear it, but it's our song, the one you sing to me. The lyrics mean so much more than you might realize.

I thought I knew you, but I can't judge you. I thought you knew me, but underneath I'm, well, not laughing but . . . different?

The lyrics don't tell the whole story, obviously.

What it deserves—what *I* deserve—isn't a quiet night. Not anymore. I thought I did, but I know now that it only makes the noise in my head grow louder.

This is my choice. My journey. Only mine. I'm heading back alone.

Nightswimming

They were floating. It didn't feel the least bit
like real life. Twelve years—thirteen, counting kindergarten.
An eternity, now in the rearview.

Trevor's hand was out the car window, a dolphin swimming away from Sutton High through the muggy June air.
Sarah was driving, as always. And as always, she was driving
the Toyota Tercel, a family car passed down two years ago
when her older sister, Janine, departed to Tufts. Janine had
called it the Silver Bullet, but Sarah referred to it as the Rat. A
demotion on account of rust and dents and stains? Perhaps. It
was a loving name, though. The Rat was a survivor. It had seen
Sarah through so much. Long detours in the farmlands after
her multiple breakups with Mike. Road trips to Rochester and
Vermont to see Phish. Predawn journeys to basketball practice
and late-night commutes home from the job at Wegmans. And
of course, the drives to school.

To school and from school, every weekday for the last two
years. For the final six months of senior year, Trevor joined her,
proudly sitting shotgun. An assorted list of guest stars rode in
the back. Jared, Schultz, and Bev had once been the other reg-
ulars. The core. But ever since Bev saved up and got a Civic in

March, those three usually rode together. Separately. Like today.

Yes, today it was only Sarah and Trevor. They both preferred it that way, even if they were both hesitant to admit it.

"Wow," Sarah said as she shook her head in disbelief.

"Wow what?" Trevor asked.

"Just wow. It's over, huh? That's it."

"Yeah. I mean . . . yeah."

What else was there to say? Class of '94 had made it. Graduation ceremony was still to come, but school was D-O-N-E done. Regents requirements met. AP tests in the books. Everything . . . complete. Trevor had prepared for it, talked and thought about it constantly, but now that it was here, he didn't know what to do.

So, he turned on the stereo. A mix was in the deck, one that Sarah made called *Sun / Rain*. One side had songs with *Sun* in their titles. The other side, *Rain*. It was on the Sun side. The Sun side always got more play.

When that fat old sun in the sky is falling . . .

Trevor let the music do the talking for a while, as they passed the fields on Sudbury, all dusty and bulldozed, ready for development. Soon enough construction would start. Houses with pastel paint jobs, flimsy transplanted trees, and in-ground pools would erupt from the weeds, though probably not before Trevor would leave for college. When he returned home next summer, however, he'd be coming back to a slightly different world.

"What time does Schultz's party start?" Trevor asked.

"Already started," Sarah said. "I saw them pouring Zimas into Sprite bottles at lunch, then heading for the parking lot."

"Should we go straight there?"

Sarah reached over to Trevor's thigh and gave it a pat—mostly fingertips—and paused for a moment to look at him before saying, "Yeah, straight there."

The driveway was already clogged with cars, so Sarah parked along the road. From the knee-high grass, she plucked a dandelion that had gone to seed and blew it at Trevor, but the wind stole the fluff before it could hit his face.

"Boooo," she said. "I wanted to fuzzify you."

"Did you at least make a wish?"

"Obviously. Now come on." She grabbed his hand and pulled him toward the backyard. The Schultz house was the last one on a dead-end road, way out past the water treatment plant, where the neighbors were too far away to complain and the cops never bothered to go. There were a few dozen kids there already, mostly in the yard. On the deck, Andrew Schultz reclined on a ratty-cushioned chaise lounge.

For lack of a better word, Andrew was an odd-looking kid, with a nose that was crooked from being broken more than once (basketball, bike accident) and bulging eyes that bordered on amphibian. But what Andrew—or Schultz, as he was known to his peers—lacked in conventional attractiveness, he made up for in charisma. Pictures of him rarely did him favors. Meeting him, however, changed almost everyone's tune. He was a disarming flirt. The young female teachers at the school knew better than to humor his advances, but they weren't immune to them. Blushing around Schultz was common. So too was smiling. He was forever welcoming, the consummate host.

As Trevor and Sarah approached the deck, Schultz raised a red plastic Pizza Hut cup in salute. "My fellow graduates. We did it!"

"Barely squeaked by, huh?" Sarah said.

"Don't joke," Schultz said. "It was touch and go for me last year. Physics was kicking my ass."

"And yet you got into Cornell," Sarah said. "Strange how that happens."

"Greatest comeback story of the twentieth century," Schultz said with a shrug.

Trevor and Sarah joined him on the deck, where they too could lord over the revelers. The party wasn't wild by any stretch of the imagination. But the smell of weed was in the air. A keg nested in a plastic tub of ice near the toolshed was already well on its way to empty.

"Your parents?" Trevor asked Schultz.

"At the lake until Sunday," Schultz said. "Plenty of time to clean up after these . . . lovely people."

"Speaking of lovely people, where's the illustrious Miss Beverly Gleason?" Sarah asked.

Schultz pointed with his thumb to the screen door behind them.

"Well then, it's been a pleasure, gents," Sarah said as she slid the door open and slipped inside.

Schultz turned his head to watch her, and when she was safely out of earshot, he said, "So?"

"So?" Trevor responded.

"You and Sarah. Is that, like . . . ?"

"Friends. That's it."

"Right. Right."

"It is right," Trevor said. "She's . . . a free spirit."

This made Schultz laugh. Hard. "That she is."

Trevor had no response, so he grabbed a seat in a nylon lawn chair, and the two guys quietly took in the crowd. More kids arrived. Trevor knew every face and voice. Sutton High wasn't tiny, but it wasn't big. Ninety-six seniors were graduating, which was two fewer than the ninety-eight who had started in September. Katie Crease had dropped out after giving birth in November. She had to find a job because her parents refused to support her and the baby, but she was well on her way to a GED. Clint Hoover had been arrested in April for stealing car stereos, and then stopped showing up at school. There were rumors that he was joining the army, but Trevor had seen him a few weeks before, manning the register at the mini-mart. They didn't make eye contact.

Katie and Clint weren't at the party, of course, but a good percentage—maybe thirty—of Trevor's fellow graduates were there. Plus, a handful of former juniors and sophomores. When Trevor spotted Jared Delson near the keg, he got out of his chair.

"Check ya later," Trevor said to Schultz, quoting their favorite movie.

"Check ya later," Schultz echoed.

Then Trevor was off, weaving through the crowd, nodding hellos at acquaintances, raising an invisible glass to friends in the distance, until he was finally standing next to Jared by the keg. Jared had a Solo cup in his hand. Trevor tapped it with a finger.

"You're drinking now?" he asked.

"Diet Coke," Jared said, and then he patted himself on the belly. "Don't want people to think I'm the new Katie Crease."

"You look fine," Trevor said, and he meant it. Jared was a skinny guy with long blond bangs that hung over his face. Skater's bangs. He looked a lot like Tony Hawk, and so he played the part, sometimes well, of idling around parking lots and public buildings, attempting kickflips and rail slides. In a hope to indulge his passion, his mom and dad once offered to build him a half-pipe in the family's barn, but he declined. "I'll be the one who's responsible for breaking my own neck, thank you very much," he told them.

It was not the response they wanted to hear, and yet it was a response that fit Jared to a tee. It spoke to his independence. Also, to his darkness, a looming presence that Trevor often wished he could chase away from his friend. Out there, in the corner of Schultz's lush and lively yard, Trevor tried to do just that. Putting his arm around Jared, he told him, "We're gonna make this the best summer of your life."

This lifted the kid's spirits, or maybe he pretended that it did. "We goddamn better," Jared said with a smile.

Twenty minutes later, Trevor and Jared were in the house, in the kitchen, sitting on the green Formica countertop, under shellacked oak cabinets. They were providing commentary as Sarah and Bev made messy sundaes.

"Add some ketchup," Trevor said.

"No, sardines. Sardines!" Jared cried.

Obviously, the girls weren't following the boys' suggestions, but they were amused.

Bev, the closest thing Sarah had to a best friend, was topping her sundae with a dollop of whipped cream from a can and then holding the nozzle below her mouth.

"Should I?" she asked.

Sarah grabbed the can from her before she could proceed. "Whippits are so stupid."

Bev shrugged. "I don't need the headache anyway."

Sarah put a blast of cream on the top of her sundae and then spooned a bite into her mouth.

Jared said, "It probably needs some olives and some—" but a booming voice interrupted him.

"Everyone on the floor! You're busted!"

Quick as quick, the boys hopped down from the counter, and the girls nearly dropped their sundaes. That was when Buck, who looked like a guy you'd call Buck, started laughing and said, "I'm messin' with you."

He was standing in the foyer, flanked by Heather and Lori, his constant companions. Heather, enamored of barrettes and black eyeliner, supplied the weed, and Lori, averse to small talk and eye contact, supplied the ride. Buck always knew where the party was, but never arrived early. Dramatic entrances were his forte.

"Don't scare us like that!" Bev said as the trio entered the kitchen. She set her sundae on the counter and slapped Buck on the shoulder. Then she gave him, and each of the girls, a hug.

Buck: bear hug. Heather: diagonal embrace. Lori: unenthusiastic shoulder squeeze.

Everyone liked Buck. How could you not? A tall and doughy dude, his voice boomed with vigor and was simultaneously deep and comforting in a way that rivaled any gregarious grandpa. His smile was genuine. He loved a good joke, but never a cruel one. His humbleness bordered on a charming cluelessness. In short: a good guy. Which made his friendship with Heather and Lori all the more confusing. The reason? Quite simply, these girls were not beloved. At least not by Trevor and his friends. Particularly not by Sarah, who harbored a deep distrust of Heather that Trevor didn't fully understand. So it came as no surprise that as the three new guests moved through the kitchen, it was Buck who garnered the attention.

"Buck," Trevor said with a nod.

"Señor Buck," Sarah added.

"Buckaroo," Jared hooted.

"This an ice cream social or something?" Buck responded. "We didn't just graduate eighth grade, you know."

"Speak for yourself, because I'll have some of that ice cream," Heather said, snatching a spoon and a tub of mint chocolate chip from the counter. She didn't bother with a bowl, just dug right in.

"You guys hitting any other parties tonight?" Jared asked.

A common question. This crew rarely stayed too long in one place.

"I heard some DH kids are out on River Road, but that'll be swarming with baseball pricks, and I'm not sure I'm up for that tonight."

Lori groaned. "Definitely not what I'm up for."

"Our chauffeur has spoken," Heather said through a mouthful of mint chocolate chip.

Buck shrugged and asked, "Where's the keg?"

Sarah motioned with her chin toward the backyard.

Buck said, "Giddy-up," and then headed that way.

"Throw Schultz some change if you could," Sarah called out to him. "He's paying for this all by himself."

Heather gave a contemptuous snort, put the tub of ice cream under her arm, and followed Buck.

Lori said, "Sorry, they're mooches," shrugged—*but what am I gonna do about it?*—and followed Buck too.

As soon as the trio was outside, Jared said, "Quick, hide all the rope." He pantomimed a noose and a hanging. Fist up, head tilted, eyes closed, tongue out.

The kitchen fell silent. Sarah's eyes went wide, and Trevor, embarrassed, turned away. Bev finally said, "Jesus, Jared. That's disgusting. Why would you say that?"

"Just saying what we're all thinking," Jared said, opening a cabinet in search of snacks.

"I wasn't thinking it," Trevor told him.

"Lori is on medication now," Bev said. "She's seeing a therapist."

"More power to her," Sarah said. "If there's any time in our lives to be happy, now is it. Hope she can enjoy it."

"Not everyone is thrilled to be done with high school," Bev said.

"Those people deserve this town, then," Jared said. "As soon as I make it to Virginia, I'm not looking back."

"Sutton too small for you now?" Sarah asked.

"Too big. Gimme a cabin in the woods. Hermitting is the life for me."

"Kermitting is the life for me," Sarah shot back, in a pretty good Muppet impression.

Everyone laughed.

By nine thirty, the sun was down, and colored Christmas lights were blazing. Fireflies sparked near the foxtail at the edge of the lawn. Eddie Vedder wailed from a boom box. There were close to sixty kids at the party, and it showed no signs of slowing down.

Trevor found a quiet spot near a willow tree, a place artificial light didn't reach. He unfolded a lawn chair and sat. He sipped a sudsy beer. It was his fourth, and there was a sizzle in his skin. A lightness. An optimism.

It was easy for him to forget the person he had been when he started high school. Skinnier, shorter, sure. Also naïve, but everyone was. It was more about beliefs. Back then he believed nothing was possible. It wasn't pessimism exactly, because he also didn't predict a future of doom for himself. He simply couldn't picture *any* future. Graduation was so far off that it might as well have been deep in the cosmos. It was beyond his abilities to imagine such a journey. Which was enough to imbue high school with a background buzz of anxiety, emotional tinnitus that he could only drown out by making sensible choices and staying busy. Sports. The school newspaper. Extra-credit projects. More recently, hanging out with Sarah. Day in and day out, these things propelled him toward that impossible destination without giving him a chance to think about what it actually meant to reach it.

Now that the journey was complete, it felt climactic. Cathartic. Many of the ways it was supposed to feel. Now that it was sinking in, it also felt entirely natural. Normal. And that buzz of anxiety? It was gone.

How long would this normal last, though? Would the buzz come back as soon as he arrived at college? Would the future be a blank slate once again? It seemed likely, but he wasn't going to dwell on that at the moment. At the moment, his focus was entirely on the figure, swaddled in darkness, that was approaching him. He recognized who it was. By her posture, her stride.

"Hey, now," he said to Sarah.

"Been looking for you," she replied.

"I've been hiding from you."

"Really?"

"No. But I could've."

"I'd hunt you down, Trev. No escaping me."

"You're probably right."

She sat in the grass.

He stood up and motioned to the chair.

"Aw, your chivalry is noted. But I'm fine."

"Fair enough," he said, and he joined her on the ground.

"Actually, I'm gonna be a total bitch and ask you to stand right back up."

"Because?"

"Because I wanna show you something."

Trevor's eyes went wide, and maybe he blushed, but it was too dark to know for sure. "Ummm . . ."

"Not like that," Sarah said.

Sarah and Trevor sauntered along the gravel road away from the Schultz house. Cicada chirps were now louder than the music. The air was humid and still. They weren't holding hands, but they were so close that they could've been.

They'd made it a few hundred yards without saying much of anything. Trevor's mind was full of possible proclamations. He wasn't sure which, if any, he should make. But it was Sarah who broke the silence.

"Why weren't we friends before November?"

Trevor kicked a hunk of tree bark off the road. "One of those things."

"We were in all those classes junior year. I always knew you were smart. Confident. Funny. And yet . . ."

"I had soccer and the paper taking up all my time. You had . . . ?"

"Basketball? Naw. I sucked. Never practiced at home. I think I was too busy hiding under the covers listening to sad songs and looking at the ceiling."

"You too?"

"I perfected it, though. I'm the master of melancholy."

She wasn't. Not even close. And she did a pirouette right there on the road that proved the point. Not a good pirouette, but a joyous one. It made Trevor smile, but he tried to hide the smile by walking ahead. And yet, even when he was ahead of Sarah, he felt behind. Emotionally, at least. It didn't have anything to do with what she said or did. It was simply about how she carried herself. Nothing seemed to faze her. She never seemed particularly stressed by school or typical teenage worries of social status. In fact, she seemed immune to existential crises of any sort.

After all, she (and the Rat) had been in an accident once. More than a fender bender. It wasn't her fault. In April, some cataract-plagued old man ran a red light and smashed her driver's-side door. Insurance paid for the repair, and she wasn't injured, thank god. But she also wasn't sufficiently traumatized. Started driving again immediately. Got right back in that saddle, as they say. Which was baffling to Trevor. He had absolutely no involvement in the accident, but it certainly affected him. For weeks his heart fluttered whenever she drove them through an intersection. Perhaps hers did too, but she never made any indication that it did. At the very least, she seemed so much better at hiding her true self than Trevor.

"Besides working, your summer is completely free, right?" Sarah said as she caught up to him.

"I'm going camping with Dan the weekend before I leave," Trevor replied.

"You still talk to him?" she asked.

"A little bit," Trevor said. "I mean, we haven't really hung out since last summer when he started dating Paige."

"Does that still hurt? It would have to, right?"

Trevor shrugged. But yeah, it did still hurt, a little. Mostly because he liked Paige. She probably would have been fine with Dan hanging out with Trevor more. The two guys had been friends for so long, and she didn't seem like the jealous type. Problem was, Dan could be intense, preferring to focus his attention on one person at a time. That person used to be Trevor. Now it was Paige. Simple as that.

"Who set up the camping trip?" Sarah asked.

Trevor raised a hand: guilty. "Thought it was the least I could do to, you know, say goodbye before college. Officially, I mean."

"So, is it real camping or fake camping?"

"What's the difference?"

Sarah jumped in front of him and put a palm up like a traffic cop. "Are you just driving to a campground and pitching a tent?"

Trevor considered his response before asking, "Is that fake camping?"

"Unless you're carrying all your gear on your back, it's fake, my friend." Then she stepped to the side and presented him with a path to follow.

Trevor stayed where he was. "How far do we have to carry it? You know, to be *not* fake?"

Sarah bit her thumb. "How about . . . more than two miles?"

"That's not a real rule," Trevor said, his chin up in defiance.

Sarah waved a dismissive hand as she turned away— "Whatever, fake camper."—and she took the lead.

When Trevor was by her side again, he said, "I don't want to go. If that makes a difference."

"Why's that? Camping can be fun. You can eat freeze-dried beans and get rained on."

"I'll miss this."

"What? We're not doing anything."

"I don't know. I just like . . . these nights."

Sarah stared at him for a moment, as if trying to read a message behind Trevor's eyes. Did she even need to look at him, though? He was clearly telling her. There was nowhere else in the world he would rather be.

Whether that's what she heard, or saw, or felt as well, he wasn't sure. But she winked. Then turned. Finally pointed down the road to a house. "Lights are off at the Rogers place. No cars there either. Pool is full."

"So?"

Sarah tossed her T-shirt into the grass and stood poolside in mismatched bra (black) and panties (green with purple polka dots). The pool was jellybean shaped and the lights were off, so the water was dark. Appeared to be more pond than pool. Pond was good enough for Sarah.

"Here goes nothin'," she said, pinching her nose. Then she counted to herself—"three, two, one"—and jackknifed into the deep end. It was a few seconds before she surfaced, but when she did, she was beaming. "You gotta get in."

Trevor stood at the edge of the pool. Shirtless, arms crossed, but with shorts still on. He never thought of himself as an ugly person, but he rarely considered himself one of the better-looking guys in school. Sure, he was an athlete, but not a toned or chiseled one. His naked torso revealed the beginnings of a potbelly and scattered tufts of wiry chest hair. His arms were skinny, but his legs were muscular, thanks to all the soccer. Every once in a while, when the lighting was favorable and his thick dark bangs were swooping just so and his face was sprouting the ideal amount of stubble, he'd look in the mirror and see a version of himself that he thought was attractive. Yet he was never quite sure if this version was attractive to girls. Or to specific girls, to be more accurate.

"What's the matter?" Sarah asked, flipping back her hair and creating an arch of droplets in the moonlight.

"Nothing," he said, looking down at the water and being thankful there wasn't enough moonlight to reveal his reflection, an image he was certain wouldn't give him the confidence he needed.

She pointed at his khaki shorts. "I know you wear tighty-whities, Trevor. If you don't want anyone to know, invest in a belt."

The teasing didn't sting too much, because he could tell it was a flirty tease. Still, he was feeling fragile enough that he didn't want to hear any more of it. Did he fear that he'd be dubbed a coward by a girl who was anything but? You bet. Which was enough to motivate him.

Okay, he told himself. *I'm doin' this.* Then he unbuttoned his shorts and quickly wiggled them down to his ankles. One foot out and then kicked them off to the side. His tighty-whities were quite tight and quite white. Even in the dark that was clear.

He didn't give Sarah a chance to bask in their glory. He dove in.

Sarah hooted and clapped in appreciation.

Twenty minutes later, they were in the shallow end, sitting, backs against the pool wall, musing at stars.

"What's the penalty for trespassing these days?" Trevor asked.

"The legal penalty?"

"I guess."

Sarah closed her eyes. "The Rogers wouldn't call the police."

"Do you know them?"

Sarah kept her eyes closed. "Don't have to. They're the Rogers. If they're called the Rogers, then they must be nice people, right?"

Trevor rolled his eyes, for no one's benefit but his own,

then moved to the deep end and slid underwater. Down there, hardly any light got through. No moon. No stars. A deep green-black. He curled up and sank for a while, let the water hug him.

When he was out of breath, he surfaced and found that Sarah was out of the pool, sitting at the edge, toes drawing designs on the water. "You ever read that Cheever story?" she asked. "'The Swimmer'?"

Trevor's fingers swept water from his face. "Mr. Ainsworth loved Cheever. All Cheever and Carver first marking period."

"But did you read 'The Swimmer'?" she asked, kicking a little water at him.

Trevor shrugged. "They all blended together."

"It's the one about the guy who swims across his town."

"Does he live in Venice or something?"

This cracked her up. "No, just a boring place like Sutton. He goes from house to house, swimming in people's pools until he makes it home."

It sounded familiar to Trevor, but he still couldn't be sure he'd read it. And yet he said, "Right, right, it was depressing," because all those stories were.

"It didn't have to be," Sarah said. "Couldn't it be awesome?"

"What?"

"Swim all the pools in Sutton."

"I mean . . . I don't know."

"Remember when I went to Chicago last month? The plane flew over Sutton on descent. I noticed at least thirty pools. In-ground ones, I mean."

That sounded about right to Trevor. Sutton wasn't exactly Florida. People had pools, but they were relatively rare.

"You're serious?" he asked.

"Would you do it with me?"

"You're seriously serious."

Sarah smiled. "We've got like what . . . a couple months before you ship off to Amherst? Average four or so a week, and we'll get it done. Hell, we've already knocked one off the list."

Trevor tried not to smile back, but he had to smile. They were right next to each other. They'd never kissed before, but this was the moment to remedy that oversight. He didn't care about her "boyfriend," if you could even call Mike that. They'd broken up so many times, it was impossible to know when they were officially together.

So Trevor tilted his head. And Sarah tapped a finger on his nose.

"Not today," she said. "But someday."

Then she slipped back down under the water.

The burning trees are a crowd gone mad, a red mob of flailing arms and musky breath, blaming me for all of it. For ALL OF IT.

I'm not to blame. I didn't start that fire. When I left, the forest decided to leave too. Better to burn out than fade away.

Now I need to run from it. That's what I do, right? That's who I am? I run?

I run.

When I know it's not working, I keep moving. It's not a bad thing necessarily. Beats lurking, fidgeting, waiting, hoping for what isn't there and never will be. Because when you run, it's always toward something.

Something better? God, I hope so.

My Drug Buddy

There was a food court at the Center Ring Mall, on the floor beneath a shiny new sixteen-screen movie theater. It was serviced by an octagonal glass elevator and boasted a Sbarro, a Happy Dragon Chinese restaurant, a Burger King, and a Cinnabon. This is where Trevor, Jared, and Schultz planned to meet for lunch every Monday and Wednesday through the summer. Trevor worked at Radio Shack, and Jared toiled away at American Eagle. Both had maintained steady hours since the fall, to save up for college expenses. Schultz didn't have a job. He was a self-proclaimed "man of leisure."

They were eating burgers on the Monday after the party at a table overlooking the atrium.

"So . . . the other night?" Schultz said to Trevor. "Details."

"None to be had," Trevor replied.

"Bullshit," Schultz said, and he threw a fry at Trevor. It bounced off his chest and onto the table. Luckily it didn't have any ketchup on it. "You two were gone for a long time."

Trevor shrugged. "Guess she doesn't like me that way. I'm not Sarah's type."

"What's her type?" Schultz asked.

Sarcasm was Jared's crutch, but also his wings. He flexed

his insubstantial biceps, flared his upper lip, and said, "It's me, right? I'm *sooo* her type."

"Nope," Trevor responded. "Older."

"Can't help that," Jared said.

"Wiser," Trevor added.

Jared winced. Fair enough.

"But there's no one wiser than you, Trev. I've seen your AP scores. Five on history. A legend in the making," Schultz said, and he reached across the table to scuff Trevor's hair like he was a little kid. But he wasn't teasing. There was a genuineness to Schultz, an earnestness that seemed, at times, condescending. It was the opposite of that. He cared deeply about his friends.

"Mike Nelson is wiser," Trevor replied, nudging Schultz's hand away. "He's got a year at Geneseo under his belt."

Schultz brushed it off. "No, man. You're plenty wise. You're like Yoda."

"We're not talking about looks," Jared said.

Trevor didn't attempt a Yoda voice, but he experimented with some Yoda grammar. "Off you must fuck now, Jared. And happening with Sarah, it is not."

Jared delivered his review. Thumbs-down. Which, to be fair, was his take on almost everything. Jared's negativity didn't make total sense to Trevor. Good grades, good-looking, good parents. What was there to be so pissy about? Perhaps the state of the world? While Trevor wouldn't exactly call Jared politically active, he would certainly call him politically astute. Jared knew in-depth details about things like "Iran Contra" and "greenhouse gases," or at least he sounded like he did whenever he brought them up in social studies or earth science. He was the first kid Trevor knew who listened to Rage Against the Machine and would often talk about his desire to attend protests like young people did in the '60s. Never followed through, though. Which wasn't surprising. City halls seemed immune to picket lines since at least the days of the Exxon *Valdez*.

Schultz, on the other hand, was an unquestionable cheerleader. "Don't sell yourself short, man," he told Trevor. "You went for a big, long walk with Sarah. Anything could've happened out there. Only took me ten minutes with Heather."

"Wait, what?" Jared said.

Schultz nodded enthusiastically. "In the basement. On the futon. After everyone went to bed."

Trevor put up a hand. "Stop it. I sit on that futon when we watch movies. I don't wanna hear this."

"Sure you do. Play your cards right, and you'll get ten minutes too. Maybe even fifteen."

While, yes, Trevor wanted those fifteen minutes, what he wanted most with Sarah was that incalculable connection. The confirmation that when the two of them weren't in the same place, she was thinking about him. The assurance that when he called her house and she wasn't there, she'd call him back as soon as she was through the door. He wanted the title: Boyfriend. Not to brag about it, but to luxuriate in it. Maybe that was why a kiss was so important. It would be a signal that she wasn't spending time with him simply because she enjoyed his company. It was because it was a compulsion, both mental and physical. After all, that's how it felt to him. It had felt that way for months. A wonderful feeling. Also, a lonely one. At least for now.

Swim every pool in Sutton? It sounded dangerous and stupid and exactly the opposite of the type of thing Trevor should be doing. They could get hurt. Or worse, arrested. He'd come this far without screwing his life up. And yet . . .

"I don't know what'll happen with Sarah," he told the guys. "But I know I'm not gonna squander any more moments I have with her."

"Attaboy," Schultz said.

"Best summer of our lives, right?" Jared said, raising his soda in toast.

Tapping the waxy rims of their cups made it official.

The week started slowly. Work. Work. Work. Dinners at home. A movie out on Wednesday, a second screening of *Speed*, which Trevor enjoyed almost as much as the first time. Keep the bus going fifty-five miles per hour or you explode. A metaphor for high school.

The graduation ceremony was the next afternoon. Thursday at the state college. In the field house, in case of rain. It didn't rain. But it was so hot that Trevor was sweating under his robe. He wasn't even wearing a shirt. Just Umbros and Chuck Taylors.

The valedictorian, Cynthia Bayliss, gave a nice speech. Not great, but nice. About new doors opening, and worlds of opportunity and whatnot. The superintendent bored the crowd with some advice about "shared social responsibility." And everyone's favorite English teacher, Mr. Frick, had countless people in tears with a story about nursing a wounded deer back to health and then setting it free in the wild.

Afterward, the newly minted graduates spent time with their families. That meant surf and turf at the Cooper Club for Trevor. He spotted other classmates in crooked ties and floral dresses, and they traded congratulations. His mom slid a glass of chardonnay across the table to him but stole it back the moment he took the tiniest sip. Wouldn't want the waitress to see. Even though the waitress, who sighed before listing the specials, obviously couldn't have cared less.

It wasn't until Friday night that Trevor saw Sarah again. And it wasn't until Friday night that they started their quest.

The Rat was parked under a tree, shielded from the street-lights. Trevor and Sarah crawled through the grass soldier-style until they were behind a row of azaleas and certain that no one would see them. Then they sprinted toward their destination: the Armstrongs' pool. Trevor wore trunks and had a towel over his naked shoulders. Sarah wore a bikini and a backpack. Their next obstacle was a chain-link fence.

"We're really doing this, huh?" Trevor asked.

Sarah tossed her backpack over the fence, then grabbed Trevor's towel and draped it over the top. "We are most certainly doing this," she said as she climbed over.

When she was on the other side, she wrapped her fingers around the chain links. A frenzy of fright overtook her eyes.

"What is it?" Trevor asked. "Did someone see us?"

She shook her head slowly. "No," she whispered. "Wolves, Trevor. There are wolves on your side. Hurry."

He didn't bother to look over his shoulder. He just smirked and said, "Fine." Then started to climb the fence too. "You're gonna get us both arrested."

Sarah considered this, and said, "Or killed. The Armstrongs have a whole buncha guns."

Joking? Probably. But Trevor stopped climbing for a moment.

"Uzis mostly," she went on. "They're Uzi enthusiasts, the Armstrongs."

"I hate you," Trevor said as he finally hopped over the top and landed next to Sarah.

"That's so not true," she responded, and she grabbed her backpack and hurried toward the dark pool. "Ya love me."

The words sounded inconsequential—and maybe Sarah meant them to be—but Trevor felt them physically. A jolt through his body. She wouldn't have noticed. She was too busy slipping into the water.

After taking a moment to collect himself, and his towel, Trevor followed.

Sarah floated on her back. Trevor swam breaststroke. Inside the Armstrong house, there was one light on, but it was a dim bathroom light. It was one o'clock. Odds were good that everyone was asleep. But Trevor still whispered.

"Schultz was pushing me for dirt about last week," he said. "You know, concerning our . . . field trip away from the party."

Sarah filled her lungs to keep her torso afloat and tried to speak through her teeth and not let too much air out. "What ya tell 'im?"

"That we went for a walk. That's it. If I ever let him know about this swimming thing, he'll try to follow us."

"Throw 'im off our scent."

"I'll leave a trail of mini vodka bottles through the woods that leads to a bag of *Hustler* magazines."

Sarah laughed and sank. Then she stood on the bottom, which was over four feet deep. The water was up to her chin.

"Does this mean you're all in, then?" she asked. "Is it official? Are we swimming every pool in Sutton?"

Trevor stood too. He had a few inches on her. The water was up to his Adam's apple. "If it means we get to spend more time together, then yeah. Obviously."

A light flicked on somewhere.

Shit.

Stone-still, Sarah whispered, "Let's go."

Then they swam soundlessly to the edge of the pool and— elbow-elbow-knee-knee—they were out.

Another light came on.

Sarah, backpack over one shoulder, and Trevor, towel under his arm, ran barefoot across a front lawn and onto a sidewalk where the streetlights spotlighted them for a moment. Dogs barked in the distance.

If anyone was looking out their window, they would've seen joy on two faces, two kids absolutely loving this.

Sarah wasn't done either. She turned off the sidewalk, sped through another dark yard, and led them past another house. To another pool. Glimmering, enticing.

"Nope," Trevor said.

"Yup."

Then she dropped her backpack and ran and jumped and, legs akimbo, dove in.

She swam the length and climbed out.

She returned to fetch her backpack.

"You're committed now," she told Trevor. "Said so yourself."

Trevor sighed. He did say that. He dropped his towel. He ran and dove in too.

When he surfaced, she held out the towel.

"Come on," Sarah said. "There are three more in this neighborhood."

Music streamed out the open windows of the Rat.

Wet hair clinging to her cheeks, Sarah drove. A hand over his eyes, Trevor laughed.

The flames stop. Like they've slammed into an invisible wall. The trees in front of me are plump and green. Behind me it's char and ash. I search back there for signs of life.

You feel miles away, but I can see you. In the water.

I can hear you. Calling out my name.

You're safe. Thank god. I should've known you would be, but seeing it convinces me to press on.

In moments—seconds it feels like—I'm through the trees and out on the other side. Past even a hint of heat or smoke. Past you.

It's suddenly peaceful. The stars are here, but they're fading. Morning is coming.

Did the others feel this way too? Defeated? Elated? Absolutely terrified?

I'm actually doing this.

Been Caught Stealing

Seven weeks. At least one night a week. At least three pools a night.

Tiptoeing when needed. And whenever possible, splashing and slapping the water and spraying each other and launching themselves gracelessly from diving boards.

Ticking off boxes on a paper map that would always end up damp by the end of the night. The poor thing was starting to rip at the folds, but they were hitting their targets, faster than planned. It would survive the mission.

Oval pools. Rectangular ones. Shapes that didn't have names.

As deep as twelve feet. As shallow as an inch of leafy, buggy rainwater. Didn't matter. A pool didn't have to be full. Barefoot puddle-stomping counted.

It was fun. Constant thrills, fueled by the realization that they were getting away with it. But there wasn't much time to lounge and talk or reflect on things. Even during the getaway drives. As they got better at sneaking into pools, their obsession with perfection became their singular focus. The only discussions were about the next strike. About adjustments to the plan and the roads to flawless execution.

The roads had bumps. Night owls lounging on decks with drinks and cigarettes, necessitating postponements. Unforeseen pricker bushes leaving nasty red streaks on their bare legs. Snarling dogs and, in one case, overly curious llamas.

But the two were persistent and careful, and they didn't view anything as impossible. They were lucky too. No police sirens. No neighborhood watch sounding the alarm. No screaming owners brandishing baseball bats.

And alas, no kiss.

I hear a hum and look over my shoulder. There are eyes on me for a moment, but then they're gone, whizzing past in the dark.

Fuck that guy.

And you know what? Fuck you too.

I'm sorry but yes, fuck you. For not leaving first. For proving you're exactly who you say you are. For telling me you'll be okay. Because you will be. You. Will be. Okay. With or without me. You always are.

And that's the problem, isn't it? I don't want okay. A weird thing to say, I know, but it's honest, and I have to be honest.

Honestly, I want . . .

I want . . .

To keep going.

Cannonball

Trevor worked. Radio Shack. Uniform. Sparse
late summer crowd. Nothing but brace-faced boys gawking at
remote-control cars and wispy-haired men sifting through
the circuit boards and transistors.

Boring, in other words. All Trevor could do was watch and
daydream. Chin in his hands, he tried to stay awake. He re-
played moments from the night before. The shimmer of the
water. The thrill of the giggles. He should have kissed her. She
had told him "someday." It should've been yesterday. It should've
been any number of yesterdays.

Someone tapped on the glass display case next to the register. "Wake up."

It was Bev.

Bev, a swirl of contradictions topped with frizzy auburn
hair. Bev, a clever and boisterous friend, but a struggling and
shy student. Bev, a flirt and a gossip who seemed scared of romantic relationships. Bev, a voracious reader of fiction and a
voracious ignorer of current events. Bev, a compassionate and
completely normal kid.

"Oh, hey," Trevor said, thumb and forefinger massaging
his eyes. When his vision cleared, he saw that Sarah wasn't

trailing in Bev's wake. Not that the two friends were inseparable, but the absence was noted.

"Got time to lean? Got time to clean," Bev told him.

"Huh?"

"That's what they used to say when I worked at Pizza Hut." Bev examined a wind-up toy robot that sat next to the register. "They were the worst."

Trevor was technically a manager-in-training at Radio Shack, but he didn't have any underlings to terrorize. His bosses were full-time managers who usually hung out in the back, which made it feel like he was working alone. Occasionally they'd try to teach him sales techniques or remind him to get phone numbers and addresses with every purchase, even batteries. Mostly they stayed back there, putting in the bare minimum, talking D&D and fantasy novels. Definitely not Trevor's preferred subjects. Sci-fi? Maybe. At least there was a logic to most of that stuff. Wizards and elves and arbitrary rules about magic were a bridge too far. Attending to customers, while often annoying, was always preferable.

"Looking to buy something?" Trevor asked Bev.

"No, looking for you."

This wasn't typical. Bev was a friend, but they didn't have a one-on-one relationship. They only interacted within the group. They didn't seek each other out for chats. There was no flirting. Trevor liked her, and he assumed she liked him too, but it rarely went beyond that.

"I'm not for sale," Trevor said.

Bev smiled, meekly but warmly, and she started to wind up the toy robot. "This is gonna be weird."

It already was. A bit. Bev popping in like this felt, not wrong exactly, but . . . weird.

"Is everything okay?" Trevor asked.

She shook her head without hesitation. Then set the robot on the display case. Its feet rotated, and it whirred and waddled a few inches, then toppled over.

"Bev?"

She sniffled, then asked, "Your mom's a nurse, right?"

"She is."

"My mom has cancer."

Trevor didn't know this. And he certainly didn't know how to respond. His grandfather had died of cancer, but his grandfather was old. Bev's mom was probably in her forties.

"Bev?" was all Trevor could think to say.

"No one else knows," she responded. "I only found out a few weeks ago."

"Oh Jesus, Bev. I'm sorry. I'm—"

"I'm telling you because maybe your mom could talk to my mom and . . . I don't know. It helps, talking, right?"

"I . . . I think so," Trevor said. "And yes. I can have my mom talk to her."

"Colorectal."

"What?"

"That's the type. I guess it's common. I don't know. They're still doing tests. Tests all the time."

"I'm—"

Bev wagged a finger. "Not another word about it. I told someone. Now I don't need to tell anyone else. At least not till I'm ready. So, no blabbing to Schultz or Jared. Or even Sarah."

"Not a word," Trevor said.

"And don't talk to me about it either. Just tell your mom to call my mom."

"I sure will."

Bev leaned across the glass case and kissed Trevor on the cheek. Then she grabbed the wind-up robot and put it in her pocket. Didn't pay. Just headed for the door. Watching her go, Trevor was amazed that her body could bear such stress, that it didn't simply crumble into a pile of ash.

Later that week, dinner at Trevor's house was shish kabobs. Beef, mushrooms, onions, and peppers. Slightly burnt, the way he liked it. Trevor's mom, Ruth, was the grill master. Grilled the meat and vegetables separately, the correct way to do it to avoid over- or undercooking. His dad, Ken, preferred to stay inside and chop the salad veggies and boil the corn.

When the meal was ready, they sat at the picnic table on the deck, the low evening sun keeping their eyes on their plates.

"So do I have to ask?" Trevor's dad said.

"What?" Trevor said.

"Ken . . . don't," Trevor's mom said.

"What?" Trevor said again.

"The Lawson girl," his dad said.

"Sarah?"

"Yeah." His dad took a bite of beef and chewed it with his mouth open. "What's the story?"

"Ken . . . ," Trevor's mom said, but what she was really saying was *let the kid have some privacy.*

Trevor played it cool. "No story. She's a friend."

"Who picks you up in her car late at night," his dad added.

"Because I don't have a license."

"And he won't need one at Amherst," his mom reminded them. "There's no rush . . . for anything."

"That's fine," his dad said, and he got up and put his hands on Trevor's shoulders. "No judgment here. Curious is all."

His dad was a tactile person. Not creepy. But the type of guy who shook your hand with two hands. Who wasn't afraid to deliver a happy slap on the back. Who kissed his son on the forehead, even if he rarely used the words *I love you.*

Trevor looked up at his dad, the sun casting a halo around his balding head. "She has a boyfriend. Michael Nelson. He'll be a sophomore at Geneseo. Where she'll be a freshman."

His dad gave Trevor's shoulders a squeeze, then released and headed for the house to get dessert. "So it goes," he called out.

Which left Trevor alone with his mom. And meant it was time to change the subject.

"Do you know my friend Bev?" he asked her.

* * *

"Marco."

"Polo."

"MARCO!"

"POLO!"

They could be loud. They knew the Reillys were away on vacation.

Trevor was it. Eyes closed, arms out, he Frankensteined toward the deep end. He suspected that Sarah was pressed up against the far edge. When the water got too deep for him to walk anymore, he started to sidestroke toward her.

The sound of ripples. She pulled herself up and out of the pool, didn't she?

The whisper of her breath as Trevor's hand grabbed the edge. Her toes were inches away, weren't they?

Silence. A moment of realization. Not only about *where* Sarah was, but *who* she was. It wasn't against the rules to climb out of the pool. It was simply risky, and rarely the best strategy, especially with only two players. A good option only when you've run out of other options. Even then, it wasn't an option that Trevor ever exercised. Which led to another realization. Or perhaps not a realization. A confirmation. Even though he had agreed to this ridiculous pool-hopping adventure, Trevor was nothing if not cautious. Always had been. And that was a good thing. His reticence to make mistakes had paid off in a rock-solid, if not spectacular, résumé, and it was the reason he was going to Amherst and she was going to

Geneseo (a fine school, but not on the same level). It wasn't because he was smarter; he knew that he wasn't. It was because big risks didn't always lead to big rewards. Some risks, many in fact, could knock you flat, could fuck your future in ways you might never imagine. Could land you at state school, in other words. At least that's what experience had told him. And for a moment, just a moment, he felt sorry for Sarah and her constant willingness to test the odds. Still, he wanted to win.

"Marco," Trevor said.

"Polo," Sarah whispered.

"Fish out of—"

She leaped over him and . . . *kersplash!*

"Sorry I didn't tell you earlier, but we can't do any others tonight," Sarah said to Trevor as they both toweled off.

"Really?"

"It's Mike. He wants me to meet a few Geneseo friends I haven't met already. So, they're having a party at his house."

"Does Mike . . . have a pool?" Trevor asked with a sly grin.

Sarah shook her head. "Even if he did, his house technically isn't in Sutton, so it wouldn't count."

"I'm guessing I'm not invited."

"No. That'd be . . . weird?"

"For him? Or me?"

"For me. Clearly."

Trevor shrugged. Nothing was clear to him anymore, especially regarding Mike.

Oh, Mike. What was there to say about that guy? He didn't hang out with Sarah's friends, which was a bit suspicious, but also understandable. Because he was in college and college guys hanging out with high school kids never seemed entirely appropriate. Even if those high school kids had recently graduated and the guy was dating one of those recent graduates. Unwritten rules and whatnot. At least for a few more weeks.

Trevor knew Mike, of course, from when he went to Sutton. Didn't know him well, though. In passing and by reputation. Mike had been a year ahead of Trevor and didn't necessarily fit into a particular mold. Played baseball, but not well. So he wasn't exactly a jock. Was part of Model UN but didn't take it too seriously. Not a stoner or a headbanger or straight edge or a computer nerd or a . . . whatever. Just a guy who drifted between social groups. People seemed to like him, and before he dated Sarah, he was with Laura Mandelbaum for a year, and they remained friends even after the breakup. That spoke to his character.

The only truly bad memory Trevor had of Mike went back to middle school and a late autumn fight on the playground when Mike was pushing dirt into some kid's face and the dirt ended up in the kid's teeth and . . . It wasn't a clear memory. Flashes, emotions, the smell of wet leaves. Maybe Mike was defending himself. Even if he wasn't, it was a long time ago. Almost every boy in middle school had been involved in a scrape or two.

The difficult truth was this. Mike was hard to hate. Fine. That didn't mean Trevor had to like him. Ambivalence could work. Trevor didn't want anything terrible to happen to the guy. But it would've been nice if he simply faded from Sarah's life, as boyfriends were supposed to do after high school. A photo left in the sun until it was nothing but a blur of color.

And yet Sarah was going to the same college as Mike. There would be no fade. They were destined to either strengthen their bond or break up in spectacular fashion. Probably after a drunken night, with one cheating on the other. Perhaps that had already happened. Perhaps that was one of the many reasons they'd broken up in the past. Sarah was cagey about so much. Especially about Mike.

It was possible that she confided in Bev. Or someone else. But with Trevor, she only mentioned Mike when emotions and bodies were inching closer to each other. It was almost always in a tone that made Mike seem like he was a cold she had to get through, or a law that was still on the books but soon to be repealed.

"So, the night is over for me, then, huh?" Trevor asked, in a tone intended to sound defiant.

Sarah squeezed water from her hair and it hit the pavement around the pool like a rush of tears. "This is not me abandoning you," she said.

"Then what is it?"

"It's me trying to figure things out."

"About?"

"About this summer. Next year. About myself."

"What's there to figure out? This is good right now, isn't it? Focus on right now."

"I'm trying, Trevor. But I'm not like you."

"What does that mean?"

"You're . . . steady."

"Steady?"

"Or . . . I don't know. I'm . . . I'm . . . I'm trying my best."

"Maybe try someone else's best, then," Trevor said at a volume just above under his breath.

It was loud enough. She spun away from him. Took a few steps. Stuffed her towel into her backpack with far more force than needed. "I'll drop you off at the bowling alley," she said. "That's where the others are."

Okay. Sure. Whatever.

Someday, she had told him. But once again, not today.

The bowling alley was mostly empty. Two employees. A young stud working the shoe counter and an old goat manning the snack bar. Some stalwarts were in the first lane. Properly gloved. Custom-made balls. Cigarettes lit and held crookedly between teeth as they rattled off strikes and spares.

At the other end, in the last lane, Bev, Schultz, and Jared played a lazy game. They were hardly keeping score. When Trevor approached them, Schultz got up first. He gave Trevor a big hug.

"Well, isn't this a nice surprise," he said. "Thought you and Sarah were off on another . . . rendezvous."

"Is she here?" Bev asked.

"Mike," was all Trevor had to say.

Schultz patted him on the shoulder and said, "Bummer, dude." Then he immediately shifted his attention to the snack bar. "Where are the nachos? I need nachos."

"They just pour Velveeta on Fritos and then dump pickled jalapeños on top, you know that, right?" Bev said as she lined up her shot.

"Sounds perfect," Schultz replied, which summed things up for him. It wasn't that he was easy to please. It was that he had figured out something that usually eluded Trevor. In short, Schultz had a keen instinct for what to let slide. Nachos were perhaps a silly example, but when Trevor heard the words "Velveeta on Fritos," his first thought wasn't *sounds perfect*. It was *sounds like a rip-off* or, even worse, *sounds white trash*. He wasn't proud of that last thought, but he couldn't deny its existence. There was also no denying that a few minutes later, when the "nachos" were plopped unceremoniously down in front of them, Trevor would pretend to reluctantly take a bite, even though he knew he'd probably enjoy them. Or certainly enjoy them enough to lick the processed cheese off his fingers rather than wipe it on a napkin. Then he'd feel guilty about it. For some weird reason, it would feel like he was being judged. By whom? Who knows.

Bev certainly wouldn't be judging him. She saved all the judgment for herself. Rolling her second gutter ball in a row, she proclaimed, "I'm *soooo* bad at this," and penciled in a big fat 0 across the scoresheet.

Making it Jared's turn. He dried his hands at the fan on the ball return, even though his hands weren't the least bit damp.

"I, on the other hand, am *soooo* good at this," he said. Then he grabbed a ball, rolled it, and knocked down four pins. Enough for him. He pumped a fist and said, "Pow!"

Across the alley, the guy at the shoe counter smiled. Jared brushed his bangs out of his face and flashed him a quick smile in return. The guy didn't go to Sutton, so Trevor didn't know him, but it appeared that Jared did. There wasn't much more to the exchange than that, a quick acknowledgment, and then Jared turned to the rack and dried his dry hands again as he waited for his ball to emerge.

"There's a party at Heather's tonight, right?" Bev asked.

"There is," Schultz said.

"So do I have to ask again if she's your *girlfriend*?" Jared teased like a middle schooler.

"She's my wife," Schultz corrected him. "We eloped last night."

Bev shrugged. "You both could do worse."

Probably true. Trevor didn't know much about Heather's dating history, other than the rumors that she hooked up with college guys. An authentic Riot Grrrl, fully equipped with a razor tongue, unkempt dyed black hair, and baby doll dresses, Heather was also a serviceable artist. She would chalk her ID and walk confidently into clubs near the college, where she'd tell everyone she was a recent grad from art school who was passing through town. It was likely she'd only done it once or twice, but it became the stuff of legend among the underclassmen who wore Metallica shirts and shared smokes by the equipment shed.

Schultz's "dating" history was a bit more documented. Whether you'd call him a playboy or a man-slut depended on your view of gender politics. In short: He got around and had been getting around longer than just about any guy Trevor knew. In middle school, he had unhooked more than a couple bras. Positively scandalous. He lost his virginity freshman year, to a junior. Seemed cool at the time, but now that Trevor was older, he knew it was a bit creepy. Especially since Schultz and the girl weren't even in a relationship. A one-time thing.

Schultz had a lot of one-time things, or two-time things, or three-time things. Never really a relationship, though. Or not more than a few weeks, in any case. Girls knew his reputation, and those who approached did so with an air of caution and a *why not? let's have some fun* attitude. He focused his attention on older girls, rarely ever hooking up with anyone younger than him, because he knew that was the quickest path to broken hearts. Surely there were people who judged him, but it was doubtful that Heather would. In the same vein, he wasn't the type of guy who'd judge a girl like Heather. So while they weren't the most obvious match, they made some sense. And yes, they both could do a lot worse.

"Congrats on the wedding," Trevor said to Schultz. "I'll buy you a fondue set."

"A fondue'll do," Schultz replied.

Jared rolled his eyes and his next ball. Two more pins down. He marked it on the nearly blank scoresheet. "Six," he said. "The highest you can get. I think that makes me the winner."

"Mind if I roll a few?" Trevor asked.

"Take over for me," Schultz said as he stepped away. "I gotta go see a man about those nachos."

Trevor stepped over to the rack, and Bev leaned in and whispered, "Your mom called. Thank you."

"No problem," he whispered back.

Heather's party wasn't really a party. Lori greeted Trevor and the gang at the door with a dour, "Join our never-ending rager, why don't you?" and then she ushered them to the basement, where four kids were draped across a sectional, watching *120 Minutes*. Heather and Buck were there. Thoroughly stoned, which should go without saying. The Brayer sisters were also making a rare appearance. Karen and Casey, both adopted, both Asian, both also thoroughly stoned. The red-eyed quartet cocked their chins in the direction of the new guests and grunted their hellos.

Lori was clearly the sober one, but when she flopped down in a beanbag chair, she essentially ignored them as well. Didn't offer seats or drinks or anything. Not a surprise, because that was exactly what Trevor expected from her. You see, Lori was easy to understand. Or she was exceedingly complicated. Depended on what you thought of her general state of dreariness. Of her hangdog demeanor. Was it an affliction or an act? A state of being or a way of pushing people away? Trevor didn't know, because he didn't know all that much about Lori. Her style wasn't distinct: She sported as many flannel shirts and baggy jeans as the next kid. She wasn't a celebrated student, or athlete, or artist. Trevor wouldn't have classified her as an unpleasant-looking person, but she had splotchy skin and split ends, and no one seemed to swoon over her. There was, quite simply, nothing especially memorable about her.

Which bothered Trevor. It was a point of pride with him that he knew a little bit about everyone in their graduating class and that he'd carry that knowledge with him into his adulthood. But he worried that after graduation, he might even forget Lori's name. For good reason. It was something he'd witnessed his parents do on more than one occasion when they'd run into an old classmate in a grocery store or at a gas station.

Obviously, no one would ever forget Schultz. He made a point of being noticed, even to a crew of disinterested pot-heads. That was why he announced, "The fun has just begun!" and strutted over to the couch, where he wiggled into a spot next to Heather. She seemed neither thrilled nor upset by this development. This had been their dynamic for the entire summer. As far as Trevor knew, they didn't go out on dates, or even hang out much alone. But gatherings brought them into orbit, and they invariably ended up crashing into each other by the end of the night. Their relationship wasn't the exact opposite of Trevor and Sarah's, but it existed somewhere in the neighborhood of opposite.

Bev and Jared were used to the arrangement by now. So they sat on the floor and didn't even bother asking Schultz if he would need a ride home. They simply watched the Meat Puppets video and shared a bag of Bugles.

Meanwhile, Trevor eased himself onto the La-Z-Boy, which had the best view of the TV, but also of the stairs. There was an open-door policy at Heather's house. Walk right in at any hour. Her mom didn't care. And Trevor was hoping Sarah might take advantage.

She could show up, tiptoe down, cheeks red from crying. She could motion to Trevor before the others would notice her. She could mouth the words, "Come on, let's get out of here." They could escape into the night, through the dark. Headlights and tears and confessions about what a jerk Mike was.

They could conquer another pool, on their backs, dark water below, starry skies above. Serene and together. Like it should be for eternity.

But that didn't happen.

Instead, the Brayer sisters nodded off. Buck made a weepy and slightly incoherent announcement about how "August is the Sunday of months," and then he and Lori stepped outside where he could smoke and vent and she could listen and nod in solidarity. Heather and Schultz snuck into the guest bedroom. Finally, Bev said, "I'm tired. Let's call it."

She drove Trevor and Jared home in the Civic, and Trevor, in the back, watched porch lights stream by and felt things he didn't like feeling. Anger? Jealousy? Something in between? Whatever it was, it made him do something without provocation. He let it slip.

"We're swimming," he said. "Every pool in Sutton. We're sneaking into people's yards at night and swimming. That's what Sarah and I have been up to."

Bev and Jared took a moment with the information.

"Kept seeing you two with wet hair," Bev said with a little laugh. "Thought you might've been showering together."

"Nope. Swimming," Trevor said.

And Jared said, "We are so into that."

"*Nightswimming deserves a quiet night,*" Sarah sang to Trevor on the phone the next day.

"That's a good one," Trevor said, recognizing the R.E.M. track. A deeper cut than some, but not exactly obscure. He was surprised they hadn't played it in the Rat yet. It was certainly appropriate.

"That's our song, buddy boy," Sarah said.

"Is it?"

"Sure is. And you ruined it."

"What exactly did I ruin?"

"*I'm not sure all these people understand,*" she sang.

"O-kay?" he said, because he didn't understand either.

"I just got off the phone with Bev. They know. They know!"

Oh. That. Trevor thought about his response. "They asked. I don't like to lie."

"Secrets are exactly the type of thing you should lie about."

"I didn't know it was a secret."

"Come on. It was our thing . . ."

True. But it was the only thing he had. While Sarah . . . she had lots of things, didn't she? With other people. This was simply one of her *many* things.

"I'm sorry," he said. "But it could be fun with more of us. It's not like we'll act any differently, right?"

Dead air, for at least a few seconds. And then . . .

"Is this about last night? About me leaving?"

"No," Trevor said, lying. "This is about sharing the magic."

More dead air. Until, with just the faintest of growls, Sarah said, "It deserves a quiet night, Trevor."

Around his waist, Jared wore an inflatable float with a dinosaur head poking up from it. Like a kid at his first pool party. It was amusing. He stood between Schultz (in running shorts) and Bev (in a one-piece), and they eyed the murky water below.

Lip curled, Bev let out a disapproving grunt. Like a dog woken early from a nap.

"You claimed you wanted to do it," Sarah said from the other side of the small, shallow, algae-laced pool.

"Yeah, we thought it'd be like skinny-dipping in the deep end of some Olympic-size waterslide dream," Schultz said. "Not some chlorine-hating hippie bog."

"Take the good with the bad," Sarah said as she slipped in. "All part of the mission."

The water went up to her ribs, and she walked carefully across the length of the pool, hands up, like she was in a swamp full of snapping turtles.

"There's a better one," Jared said. "I even know the owners. My dad works with the dad. We could get permission."

"Not getting permission is sorta the point," Sarah said as

she pulled herself out of the muck. "And if you're truly joining us, then you have some catching up to do."

"Okay," Bev said, swirling the water with a toe. "How many is that?"

"Twenty-five?" Sarah asked Trevor.

"Counting this one?" he responded. "I'd have to check the map in the car, but I think it's actually twenty-nine. Not far from the end."

"What happens when you swim them all?" Schultz asked.

"We win," Sarah said as she toweled off.

"Win what?" Bev asked.

"Life, Bev. Life."

"And if we get arrested?" Jared asked.

"We're not getting arrested," Sarah said.

Jared turned to Trevor for confirmation.

"We're careful," Trevor said. "I wouldn't be doing this if we weren't."

"Careful or not, it's still possible," Bev said.

"Just don't splash too much, and we'll be fine," Sarah said.

Schultz smirked and said, "Well, what are they gonna do to us, really? We already got into college."

Then he belly-flopped into the goop.

Dawn is threatening to break, and my mind is racing.
Options, options, endless options.

I could track the others down, ask them where they went
and what they saw. But would that help? They're different
than me, you know. They needed something different than
I did, didn't they?

Doesn't matter. Because that was then, and this is now. So,
what do I need now?

To find a bed and go to sleep, a real sleep, and see what
happens when I wake?

To hide? To run? To keep running?

I could ...

Purple Haze

They hit two more pools—the one Jared recom-mended and a lovely circular one at Deer Run, the new development near Bev's house. It was nearly midnight, but there was still time for at least one more. And there was an intriguing option on the list.

It was at the edge of Sutton, behind an old farmhouse that was painted purple. There was a purple Cadillac in the driveway, and the lights were off, except for purple-tinted Christmas bulbs that framed the front porch. Purple wildflowers choked the yard and reached almost as high as the purple plastic flamingos standing cockeyed in the earth. A purple flag flew on a purple flagpole. A theme was evident.

They parked along the road, and to everyone's relief, they didn't even have to go near the odd house. A mown path meandered through weeds and led from the road to the backyard and the pool. The pool wasn't purple—its liner was marbled blue—perhaps because no company makes a purple pool liner. But everything around it was purple. Lounge chair cushions, a free-standing archway wrapped in purple fabric, even the leaf skimmer with its chipped purple paint on the handle. Those purple Christmas bulbs were here too, lit up and draped from surrounding pines.

"Trippy," Bev whispered.

It was that. Also magical. In a cheesy way. Like something out of a cheap sword-and-sandal movie. A land of nymphs and centaurs and chiffon.

"Anyone know who lives here?" Schultz asked.

"I wonder that same thing every time I drive by," Sarah said. "But I never see anyone around."

"I have a theory about the person," Jared said.

When he didn't elaborate, Trevor asked, "Which is?"

With a piercing stare, Jared said, "They like purple."

Schultz started cracking up, and Bev put a hand over his mouth. "Cool it. We don't know if anyone is here."

"I bet it's Barney," Jared said.

"*I love you, you love me, we're a happy family,*" Schultz began singing through Bev's fingers.

"Stop it," Bev said, and she squeezed his mouth shut. "Pyper watches that shit constantly. I love my li'l stepsister, but that song is eating away at my brain."

"So, are we swimming in the lavender lagoon or what?" Sarah asked.

Trevor tested the water with a hand. Smiled and nodded.

The water temperature was lovely. Close to eighty, but entirely warmed by the sun. August was kind like that. The night air was cool, sixties, so they all tried to stay submerged up to their necks. Far warmer in than out. Not exactly a hot tub, but close enough.

There was a diving board, and Bev clung to it with one hand, so she didn't have to tread water in the deep end. "I can't believe summer is almost over," she said.

No one responded at first. It wasn't a reality any of them wanted to accept.

"This guy goes camping next weekend," Sarah finally said as she swam up behind Trevor and put her hands on his shoulders. "Then after that, he's gone."

"Really, camping?" Jared said. "That's masochistic of you."

"I set it up with Dan before graduation," Trevor explained with a sigh. "But I'd rather stay here next weekend."

Sarah's hands were still on his shoulders, and Trevor never wanted them to leave his shoulders. She gave him a squeeze and said, "So cancel and stay. You haven't even seen Dan this summer."

His guilt was double. Rescinding the invitation to his buddy felt wrong. So did ditching Sarah. But the invitation had come first. Suddenly uncomfortable, Trevor swam away from Sarah's hands. "It's true," he said. "I haven't seen Dan. But I promised Dan. And he's my oldest friend. Loyalty. That's what matters."

Sarah's head tilted, and her eyes narrowed. "Loyalty, huh?"

The subtext was also double. Dan had shown no loyalty to Trevor. And now, according to Sarah, Trevor was showing no loyalty to her. Which wasn't entirely fair. He never explicitly told her he would keep the swimming a secret. Besides, couldn't it be better this way? With more friends?

"Know what my brothers used to do in the summer?" Schultz said as he sat down in the shallow end.

"Besides beat you up?" Jared asked.

"They still do that. No. I'm talking about farmhousing."

Puzzled eyes.

"That's not even a word," Bev said.

"True," Schultz said. "Until they made it up. It's when you take people to abandoned farmhouses."

"Why would you do that?" Bev asked.

"To scare the crap outta 'em. Hazing, basically. Seniors would get a van full of freshmen and drive them out to the boonies where there are these creepy old farmhouses."

"I think I've heard about this," Trevor said. "The eighties were nuts."

Schultz pointed at him. "Yes, they were. And beforehand, the seniors would make the places even creepier. They'd spray-paint pentagrams and set up satanic stuff inside."

"Whaddya mean satanic stuff?" Bev asked hesitantly.

"I don't know," Schultz replied. "Like goat skulls and Victrolas and whatnot."

This made Sarah laugh. "Victrolas? Very satanic."

"When they're playing scratchy music from the 1920s, they're downright evil," Schultz said.

"He isn't wrong," Jared added.

Sarah laughed again. "So, Schultz and Jared are afraid of record players. Filing that information away for when they least expect it."

Bev started cracking up too, perhaps more than she should've. Had she smoked some weed earlier? Probably not. She was driving and took that responsibility seriously. Her laughter was likely the result of a feeling with which Trevor was becoming quite familiar: the joy of being just a little bit bad.

Bev's laughter, however, didn't last long. Because someone else spoke and stopped it right in its tracks. The voice was unfamiliar.

"May I join you?"

Oh shit.

A woman emerged from the darkness. At first, it seemed like a trick of the light, but as she approached the pool, it became apparent that her hair, worn up, was dyed purple, to complement her purple bathing suit and purple slippers.

It was hard to tell how old she was. Fifties? Perhaps. But she gave off an aura. She seemed . . . robust.

The kids scrambled toward the edge to get out.

"We didn't—"

"We're not—"

"This isn't—"

The Purple Woman waved them off. "Don't worry. I'm only here for my midnight dip."

They all stayed frozen where they were as she kicked her slippers to the side and stepped into the water at the shallow-end stairs.

Schultz was the first to move again, scooting out of her way as he said, "You're just gonna swim?"

"It is my pool, after all."

Bev had shimmied up onto the diving board, and was now sitting (and shivering), arms crossed, at the end. "We're not, like, criminals or—"

The Purple Woman put up a hand. "You're welcome here. I'm glad to have people enjoy the pool. I'm usually alone."

Then, with practiced grace, the woman slid into the water, keeping her head above the surface, her purple hair dry.

The gang exchanged glances: *So, is this cool? I guess this is cool.*

"What other pools have you been to?" the Purple Woman asked as she breaststroked toward the deep end.

"Excuse me?" Sarah said.

"You're not pool-hopping virgins, I'm guessing," she said as she touched the far edge and then pushed off with her feet. Her movements were as fluid and natural as a morning stretch and yawn.

Schultz raised his hand and offered up a response. "I was a pool-hopping virgin until today. They deflowered me."

That bought him an eye roll from Bev.

"Have people snuck into your pool before?" Sarah asked the Purple Woman.

"A few. And vice versa."

"What? You sneak into pools too?" Jared asked.

The Purple Woman kept up the perfect breaststroke as she said, "I did sneak into pools. Eons ago. Me and my boyfriend, Fred Flintstone."

It was the corny sort of humor Trevor was accustomed to

from his grandparents, so he'd been trained to laugh at it. The others followed suit.

And Bev said, "Well, you don't look that old, Wilma. Or are you Betty? Did Fred and Betty ever have a thing?"

The Purple Woman let out a little snort. She appreciated the willingness to stretch the joke out.

As always, Sarah and Trevor found themselves next to each other, and Sarah used it as an opportunity to announce their bond. She grabbed him by the crook of the elbow and pulled him in close. "Me and Trevor here have swum every pool in Sutton."

The Purple Woman finally stopped swimming when she reached the stairs, where she took a seat. "Every last one?" she asked.

"Close to it," Trevor said, because that was the truth. Check marks riddled the map.

"The Burton place?" the woman asked.

"Yep," Sarah said.

"Huntington Manor?"

"Oh yeah," Trevor told the woman. "We set off an alarm there."

"Been out to the natural pool off Watervale?"

"The what?" Sarah asked, and Trevor could feel her fingernails dig into him. She didn't like not knowing things.

"The natural pool," the woman said. "I think the Bennett family still maintains it."

Sarah turned to Trevor, and Trevor shook his head. No such circle on their map. "We have no idea what you're talking about," she said.

"It's in the woods. Down a dirt path near the corner of Watervale and Euclid. Your parents have never taken you?"

"My parents haven't even taken me to Chuck E. Cheese," Jared said with a theatrical sigh.

Bev, still sitting on the diving board, kicked some water at him. "Such a sad life you lead."

Puppy dog eyes in return.

"Seriously," Sarah said. "Give us the lowdown on this pool."

"I believe it's fed by a spring, but was dug by machines," the woman explained. "Not sure when. Before I was born. There are benches made from logs. Torches for light, but I heard you have to bring your own fire."

Fire they had. It was in Sarah's eyes as she turned to Trevor: *We've gotta go!*

Trevor needed more information, though. If it was near the corner of Watervale and Euclid, it was technically in Sutton. But over the summer, they had gotten better at researching their targets and pulling off their swims. Tonight was the first time they were actually confronted by an owner. That was because of sloppiness and spontaneity. He didn't want to make the same mistake twice.

"Who did you say owns it?" Trevor asked. "The Bennetts?"

"They maintain it," the woman said. "It's owned by a land trust. They make it open to the public. Funny thing is, I've never been to it, even though it feels like it was a big part of my life. Like something you hear stories about, even dream about, but never actually see. I meant to go when I was a teenager. Came close a few times, but it never worked out, for whatever reason. Now I'm too old and it's really a place for young folks, like yourselves."

Schultz stood up. "We're going, right? Tonight. We're doing this?"

Sarah beamed.

Trevor shook his head.

"Someday," he said. "But not today."

Whether Sarah knew that Trevor was echoing her— mocking her?—was unclear. But she reacted with force. "No. Now. If you're going camping with Dan next weekend, then we might miss our chance. Thanks to you, the gang's all here, and that might not happen again. So tonight. Now or never."

The Purple Lady reached up and removed a clip from her hair, which tumbled down past her shoulders. She ran her hands across the surface of the water, barely touching it but sending ripples toward the kids.

"I regret never going," she said. "But you don't have to regret anything."

"Don't worry," Sarah said, pulling herself up on the edge. "I never do."

This information pleased the Purple Lady, who closed her eyes and let out a long, satisfied hum of agreement.

"Anything else we should know?" Bev asked.

"The only other thing I'll say is this: If you want to make this night last, then make it last."

Trevor didn't want that. He was tired and still annoyed about Mike and feeling so many conflicting emotions about where and how he should be spending his last days of summer. And yet he didn't have any choice other than to follow the group. Sarah was already out of the water, keys to the Rat in her hand, shaking them as if to entice a baby.

He reached up and grabbed the lip of the pool. He felt a vibration through his body, not unlike a shiver. Whether it was his decision or not, a decision had been made. The night was taking a turn.

They were going.

I could go back.

I *should* go back.

If I can get back.

To explain. Not to apologize to you. Only to explain that this is what I need, and what I always needed. The endless quiet simply confirmed it.

Sure, I'm being selfish, but I deserve to be selfish. We all do at this point in our lives. I'll simply tell you that and leave again.

It's the least I can—

No.

Harvest Moon

The trees ate them. Headlights swallowed up in a tunnel of green. This was Watervale, the darkest road in the darkest corner of town. It wound through land that was once farmed but was now thickly forested. Land that no one wanted. Not because it was bad land. It was hilly and lovely and full of craggy rocks that sat shoulder to shoulder and formed tiny enclosures that looked like the entrances to caves. If this land were in town, it would've been overtaken by development long ago. But out here it was too much work. Too far from schools or shops or anywhere of consequence.

Trevor had been out this way a few times in the last couple years. On one of his mom's "longcuts" to Uncle Ray's camp in the Adirondacks. But never in such dark, so it felt like an entirely different place. Frightening? Not exactly. Maybe he was still too annoyed with Sarah to worry about any monsters hiding in wait. Or maybe he was too tired to care.

Bev, Schultz, and Jared had stopped for gas and snacks, so they were at least ten minutes behind, which gave Trevor and Sarah time to get the lay of the land. Sarah pulled the Rat into a patch of weeds and dirt just past the intersection with Euclid. It may have been a proper parking lot at some point; it was big enough for a few cars in any case. Which was all they needed.

Engine off, Sarah dug a long black Maglite out from under a stack of maps in the glove box. "Let's do it," she said, clicking on the bulb and pushing open her door.

The beam lashed the trees, then stabbed at a spot where the growth seemed to part, an opening into . . . Well, it was hard to say.

"There?" Trevor asked.

"Only one way to know."

Sarah rushed forth, light bobbing, and stopped when she reached a patch of bushes. She parted them with a hand and held the Maglite forehead high so she could examine within.

"A trail," she said with glee, before sliding sideways through the brush. Shoulder first, then head, body, legs, gone.

Trevor paused. It was a long, but doable, walk home. He was well aware that he could take off right then. Finish out the summer and never see or even call Sarah again. That wasn't what he wanted to do, but the possibility was present, and if he took it, could Sarah blame him for it? Not if she didn't want to be called a hypocrite. She'd done the same thing herself.

Trevor was thinking particularly about Jennifer LaSorda. Jennifer had been Sarah's best friend in middle school. To call them inseparable would've been an understatement. Even though he didn't know them well at the time, he had viewed them as a single unit, so much so that he had trouble telling them apart. They both had long, wavy brown hair. Back then, both of their mouths were a rugged landscape of metal braces.

They didn't wear matching outfits, but they shared items from their wardrobes. A sweater here, a rugby there. They referred to themselves as the Silly Sisters, though Trevor didn't view them as particularly silly. A little goofy? Perhaps. But most kids were back then.

Something changed over the summer between eighth and ninth grade. They didn't go from being friends to enemies, but they each started acting like the other girl didn't exist. Passing each other in the hall without a word. Splintering into different friend groups that didn't interact. They were never outwardly nasty to each other. They simply severed their relationship. Completely.

Sarah's trajectory in high school was one of increasing popularity. Not that she was considered some "cool kid" or Homecoming Queen or anything, but her social circles bloomed. While Jennifer's shriveled. Jennifer became dedicated to band (she played percussion) and Mock Trial and not much else. She had friends, but it was a tight-knit group. It seemed obvious to Trevor that Sarah had abandoned Jennifer.

Of course, Trevor wasn't going to do the same thing to Sarah now. He also wasn't going to scurry after her like some eager puppy. He took his time, scanning up and down the road, testing the locks on the car, watching the fingers of leaves twiddle nervously in the air. The breeze was cool, but not so cool as to remind him of winter, or even fall. His body had grown so accustomed to summer. It had basically forgotten those other seasons.

He rubbed his eyes with the heels of his hands and checked

for constellations he might recognize. Cassiopeia, the big W, was visible in a slash of sky above the road. He had learned a bit of mythology in Latin classes over the years, but the only thing he remembered about Cassiopeia was that she was the mother of Andromeda. Andromeda was up there too. An entire galaxy that, to the naked eye, resembled a single blurry star. He didn't know which dot of light it was, but he stared until they were all a little fuzzy and any of them could've been a swirl of suns and planets. Then he rubbed his eyes again.

"Wait up," he finally said as he strode toward the spot where Sarah had slipped into the wilderness.

As soon as he stepped through the curtain of leaves and onto a thin dirt trail, he was compelled to stop, to stand stiff and alert. Because someone else was there. A wiry young man—shirtless and in frayed cutoff jeans—was leaning toward Sarah, and Sarah was shining her light on his bare chest and the towel draped over his shoulders. He was whispering something to her.

Trevor managed an "Uh . . . hey," before the guy turned and cocked a chin.

"It's all yours, amigo," the man said, and he started moving toward Trevor, while Sarah kept the Maglite pointed at him.

The light on the guy's back created a corona around his thin frame, an artificial, shimmering skin. Trevor stepped off the trail, and the guy, who had a thin mustache but looked to be about eighteen years old, coursed past him. Pausing for a moment at the wall of dark green, breathing deep through his nose, and then pushing through with both hands, the young man made a somewhat exaggerated exit. Almost like he was stepping onstage for a performance or into a room to take an important test. A here-goes-nothin' moment that he had been anticipating for a long time. Or that's how it looked to Trevor. Odd, to say the least.

"Who the heck was that?" Trevor asked when he joined Sarah farther down the trail.

"Some dude. Don't know him. But he had . . . a towel!"

No one had ever been as excited by the sight of terry cloth, and Sarah couldn't contain herself. Giddy, she was off down the trail.

There were tiki torches, a few dozen dotting the edge of the natural pool, and they were all lit. Was this considerate of the shirtless gentleman? Or negligent on his part? Didn't matter. A blanket of orange hugged the water. Absolutely lovely.

The pool was bigger than Trevor expected. Beyond Olympic size. Twice as long as it was wide, and presumably plenty deep. The walls were mostly concrete, except for the spot where the spring poured in. Expert masonry, a puzzle of stone, created what amounted to a giant bathtub tap: a shelf, a channel, a little waterfall.

There was no deck to speak of. The pool was framed by a grassy lawn, which was weedy in a few spots near where it met the woods but was mostly well kept. By whom? That was hard to say. There was no mower in sight, or a shed to hold landscaping equipment. Besides the pool, there were benches made from hewn logs. A few old picnic tables. And of course, the tiki torches. The whole area was one acre? Possibly two? Enough that it seemed neither small nor sprawling.

The walk to get there had taken around five minutes, so Trevor estimated it was a quarter mile from the road. Maybe a bit farther, because they had moved fast. But it felt worlds removed from anywhere. Once they were standing at the edge, peering over the slithering reflections of torch flames and into the forest on the other side, they may as well have been looking into a wall of oil. The darkness was beyond thick. It was throbbing and viscous.

Behind them, the same. They couldn't even see the trail that had brought them there. Though that hardly mattered to Sarah. "Goddamn paradise," she said.

The grass called out to her before the water did, and she sat cross-legged in it for a few moments, then fell backward, fanned her arms out. Not quite a grass angel, but close.

"Okay," Trevor said, sitting next to her. "This is nice."

"I almost don't want to swim in it right away," she said. "I want to save it. Like the last piece of cake."

"We can't stay long," Trevor said. "I need some sleep."

"I'll pretend I didn't hear that."

They listened to something else for a while. To the bubble of the spring. It was a lullaby of sorts, the sort of sound you'd hear in a Japanese garden. Trevor was lucky he wasn't lying down too, or else he might have faded off to sleep.

"Where do you think it drains into?" he asked.

"What do you mean?"

"The pool is fed by a spring, but it's not like there's a pump or something recirculating the water. So where does it go?"

Sarah was a good student. She was also clever, which was a different thing than being a good student. But she didn't have a sufficient answer for this question. "It soaks into the ground. Or disappears into the ether. It becomes one with the night. Who cares?"

Indeed. Sarah didn't seem to have a care in the world. While Trevor cared only about sleep. He wanted to take a dip and be done with it. Go home and be dead until noon. When he was younger, he had dreamed of nonexistent curfews, of spending an entire night outside, on adventures, with a girl. A good chunk of his summer had been spent doing exactly that. The luster, at least for now, was wearing off. Or maybe it was his patience. For all his insecurities, Trevor had been fairly certain that Sarah shared at least some of his intense feelings. Now, as summer was burning to the end of its wick, he was realizing that he had probably been naïve.

He stood up. Maybe he'd run and jump into the water, then get out and insist that Sarah drive him home. Or maybe not. He wasn't sure yet.

Whatever he decided, he certainly wasn't prepared for what Sarah said next.

She sat up and narrowed her eyes. "You've been wanting something. A kiss, or I don't know, something more? I'm not dumb. It's obvious. I'm not going to apologize for not . . .

giving it up or whatever. Because it's silly, and I have my reasons. Can we at least acknowledge that? Out in the open?"

It wasn't exactly what Trevor had been hoping to hear, but it gave him a measure of relief. It meant he could ask a question too.

"Okay," he said. "You're right. But what about you?"

"What about me?"

"I know I'm not entitled to anything from you. But what do you want from me?"

Sarah paused for a moment. She couldn't have been considering her answer, because how could she have not already known her answer? Maybe she was deciding how honest she was willing to be.

"I've been told that when I'm sad, I can't sit still," she finally said.

"Oh," Trevor replied, not expecting that response. "Okay. By who?"

"Multiple people," she said. "People who've gotten to know me even better than I know myself, I guess. Because I usually don't notice it. Apparently when I'm not happy, I'm darting here and there and everywhere. Like I'm trying not to be caught."

"Caught by . . . ?"

"I don't know."

"Maybe your feelings?"

"Could be. Lately I've been trying to be more aware of how I'm acting. And feeling. Like right now, for instance."

Right now, she was hardly moving at all. Sitting there,

hands bracing her from behind, eyes locked on Trevor, mouth barely parted.

"So, do you feel happy here?" he asked.

"I feel so goddamn happy, Trevor. I need this night, this place, this moment in our lives to be . . . special. There's a reason you're the person I've been sharing my summer with. You must know that."

"But I don't know that. I'm so boring compared to you. Sometimes I don't understand why you even like me."

He could hardly believe he was saying it, but he had to say it. An insidious feeling had been coursing through his body of late, and this was the first time he could put words to it. Yes, he was impatient. But not with her. He was impatient with himself. Holding out hope was something he wasn't strong enough to do. Deep down, he feared he wasn't strong enough to do much of anything.

Sarah put a hand on his cheek and held it. Could she see that his face, and with it his entire world, was collapsing?

"Oh, Trevor," she said. "You wanna know why I like you? It's not just because you're cute, which you most definitely are. I like you because you like me. *You* like *me*. Sounds simple, but it isn't."

Her hand was right next to his lips. He could kiss the edge of her palm if he wanted to, and boy did he want to. But he wanted to hear what she had to say even more. So he just nodded, and she gave his earlobe the gentlest of pinches before peeling her hand away.

"You actually listen to me," she went on. "You smile when

I need to see a smile. You don't try to force your ideas on me, or try to impress me by introducing me to, I don't know, new bands or movies or sports. You just want me to be me. The girl who, against all good judgment, decides to swim her way out of this town. You're not boring, Trevor, because you're confident in who you are. And that makes you confident in who I am. Which I, most definitely, am not."

Trevor was hearing what she was saying, and loving what she was saying, but it didn't sound the least bit like him. Or her, for that matter. How could she not see right through him?

"You're the one who's confident," Trevor said.

Sarah shook her head, ever so slightly, and whispered, "You asked me what I want from you. I want everything. I want it all before our moment slips away. *This?* This could be everything, couldn't it? And it's bound to slip away, isn't it?"

So, did they kiss right then?

Of course they didn't. As if it were that easy. The inevitable happened.

"Ho-ly shit," Schultz said as he stepped out of the forest and into the tiki light. "This place is *amaaaaazing.*"

Jared and Bev followed, lugging plastic bags bursting with all varieties of gas station delicacies: candy, chips, jerky, cheap wine.

"We got some guy to buy us Boone's!" Bev announced. "KABOOM!"

There were at least half a dozen bottles clanging around inside two of the bags. Boozy, fruity wind chimes.

The moment with Trevor was over, so Sarah hopped to her

feet. "A toast!" she shouted as she rushed over and snatched a bottle of Strawberry Hill. But she didn't actually wait for a toast. She cracked the cap and took a long, satisfying slug. Then she brought the bottle to Trevor. "Let's swim," she said, handing it over.

It was settled. They weren't going anywhere for a while. Because if Sarah was committed to drinking, then he wouldn't ask her for a ride. And he wasn't exactly comfortable driving her car by himself, seeing that he only had his permit. Besides, he was still absorbing her deluge of proclamations. Was this place, this moment . . . was it "everything"? Even with the arrival of the others, Trevor hoped that maybe it could be. Somehow, he conjured the strength he had felt he lacked, the will to hold out hope a little longer. And that was why he took a long draw off the strawberry wine too. He didn't hate the taste, and he had no reason to believe it was awful, because he'd never had good wine. The warmth of the alcohol gave him the last push he needed.

"Me first," he announced. Because he knew asking to be first would be a lost cause.

Handing the bottle to Schultz, he ran, he jumped, he landed feetfirst in the water and . . .

No. That would be a mistake. I can't go back.

I left for a reason, and there's only one reason to go back.
It's a bad reason, the worst of them all. A different type
of selfish. False promises. False hope. And for what? A
clean conscience? A little more comfort?

No. That's cruel. Crueler than what I've already done.

It's best for you—for everyone—if I keep going.

Lithium

A fizz in his skin. A thump to his heart. The water wasn't cold. Yet it was still bracing. He stayed down long enough to feel, and hear, torpedoes all around him.

Flit. Flit. Flit. Flit.

Other bodies entered the water. He couldn't see whose, but he could guess.

Sarah. Schultz. Bev. Jared. That order. It could be no other order.

Trevor's parents had records of whale songs. A '70s fad. *Save the Whales! Because they sing!* He had to admit there was something to it, though. He would spin the vinyl and feel the feelings. A connection between species? Maybe. Something.

Mmmmwwwwaaaa.

Underwater, he sang too. He tried to copy the whale sounds, but he had no idea whether the others could hear him. Or if they did, if they recognized it as anything more than noise.

Trevor felt virile. His lungs? Huge. He could stay down for a while if he wanted to. Part of him wanted to. But he knew he shouldn't, so he surfaced.

"Yaaaaaa!"

Schultz was screaming. A good scream. A rapturous howl.

Jared echoed it. Then Bev too. Mouths agape, heads tipped back, hair skimming the water.

Sarah was silent, though. She swam up to Trevor instead. Placed her hands over his ears, stared him square in the eyes, opened her mouth, and . . .

Nothing. A voiceless scream. But joyous.

It worked. He smiled.

"Okay," he said. "We'll stay."

There were no clocks. No one had a watch. No one had even thought to bring one. Because, really, what would their parents do if they were late? Worry, of course. At least the ones who waited up might. But they wouldn't call the cops. Not until well into morning. They were teenagers once. They'd chased the dawn too.

The dawn felt years away. The dark was still so thick. And the sky was askew.

"What happened to the stars?" Bev asked.

They looked up. Not a single pinprick of light. Black.

"Or the moon?" Sarah asked.

"Probably just clouds covering it," Schultz said.

"I don't see any clouds," Jared said.

"Weird," Trevor said, and he swam to the edge.

As he climbed out of the water, he felt a tug. Not on his legs or arms. On his entire body. Like the water was a heavy blanket, coaxing him back to bed. Not strong enough to stop him, but enough that he noticed.

Weird, he thought. And he looked back up at the sky. Yep. Nothing.

The others didn't seem particularly bothered by it. They were too busy splashing and laughing. But Trevor had seen the stars earlier. Clearly. Now they were gone. Jared was right. Not a cloud in the sky.

It sparked a memory for Trevor.

His buddy Dan's house when he was a boy. Dead of night. Sneaking from the bunk bed to the study, where there was a heating vent in the floor. Placing a navy-blue sheet over it. Placing books on the corners of the sheet. Then fiddling with the thermostat until—*whoosh*—a dome. Warm and dark and oppressive and wonderful. Huddling inside until they couldn't stand it anymore. And then bursting through the hot dark roof until at least two sheet corners were free and flapping. Floating back to the bunk bed on a raft of giggles.

It wasn't the exact same feeling at the natural pool. It was similar, though. Only Trevor had no idea what was forming the dome above them. He stared for a while, looking for a crack, or a hole. A ripple in the fabric of the sky. Nothing. And as soon as he looked down, he stopped thinking about it. Not that he would know that. Which is the lovely and horrible nature of forgetting. Out of sight, out of mind.

Into sight came three figures, emerging in the glow of the torches.

"Well, well, well, what is this little slice of heaven?" Heather said as she approached.

Buck and Lori followed, with backpacks over their shoulders. "Supplies!" Buck hollered.

Sarah glared. First at Schultz. Because she put two and two together. As did Trevor. There was a pay phone at the gas station where Schultz had stopped with Bev and Jared. He certainly had the change and the time to call Heather and invite her to the secret oasis. And wherever Heather went, Lori and Buck followed.

Sarah's glare then shifted to Trevor. Because he was the one responsible for the tumble of dominos. If Trevor hadn't blabbed the other night when they went bowling, then it would be just the two of them here. Alone. Of course, Trevor knew this, but he also knew he couldn't change the past. It was better to find the positive spin. New people meant new distractions. While the others were occupied with the recent arrivals, perhaps he and Sarah could recapture some alone time. In that way, he was glad to see more people.

"Surprised you could find us," he said with a chirp in his voice.

"I thought we might get eaten by bears," Lori deadpanned.

"No Yogis and Boo-Boos around here," Buck said. "This ain't the Adirondacks, babe."

"Seriously," Heather said. "What is this place? How have I never heard of it before?"

Sarah floated on her back, eyes closed. "I guess you don't really have your finger on the party pulse of our humble little burb."

The mildest of teasing, but Heather's face took the hit. Her lip curled, her eyes narrowed, and she whispered something to herself. *Bitch?* Perhaps, but Sarah wouldn't know it. She was too far away.

Buck tromped over to the edge of the pool, skimmed the surface with his fingertips. Satisfied with the temperature, he asked, "So who brought me some trunks?"

"Your fat ass might have to skinny-dip," Schultz said.

"No one wants to see that," Jared added.

"I don't know about that," Buck said. "The ladies haven't chimed in yet."

Lori's chime came in the form of a push. Quick and devious, right below Buck's shoulders.

He tottered, then tumbled.

Splashed.

Sank.

Lori laughed louder than Trevor had ever heard her laugh. Though not sadistically. She seemed monumentally pleased with herself. Perhaps surprised by her own rambunctiousness. That is, until the young man didn't surface.

"Buck?" she said softly, eyebrows knitted.

"Buck," Heather echoed, louder, more forceful. "Stop fucking around."

Hero mode took over, and Schultz wasted no time. He dove down to rescue their friend. Almost as soon as Schultz was under, Buck emerged and shouted, "Goddamn, goddamn! So refreshing!"

Lori nearly collapsed with relief. "Why would you do that? I'm so pissed at you!"

"*You're* pissed at *me*?" Buck said with a huff. "I should be grabbing your ankle right now and pulling you in here."

No dice. Lori hopped back from the edge. "Gonna have to come and get me, Mr. Soppy Socks."

"And leave this?" he said, splashing water on his acne-scarred face. "No thank you, ma'am. This shit is magic."

"It is, isn't it?" Sarah said wistfully.

"What do you mean by that?" Heather asked. "It's warm?"

"Naw," Buck said. "It just feels . . . right. Jump in, and you'll get it."

Schultz, who had surfaced as well, nodded, and pointed to the water: *Get in.*

Heather paused. Sat down cross-legged, elbows in the pits of her knees. Pinched her fingers. Closed her eyes. Meditated on it.

"What do the spirits say?" Bev asked.

Heather opened her eyes and was matter-of-fact. "The spirits said what they always say. Removeth thy clothes."

She listened. Hopped up, kicked off her Doc Martens, peeled off her black socks. Tossed the plaid skirt and the L7 T-shirt to the grass. She remained modest for a moment, with strategically placed arms and crossed thighs. But then the rest came off too.

Jared and Trevor tried to be gentlemen, turning away, but Schultz laughed at them. "Ask her if she cares first, guys. In my opinion, it's worth a look."

"How very feminist of you," Heather said, but she didn't give the others much chance to look, because she ran and—"Cannonbaaaaall!"

Sploosh.

Even Sarah couldn't resist nudity mixed with nonsense. While she wasn't the biggest fan of Heather, she was a fan of this. It showed true commitment to the cause.

She clapped and shouted, "Now that's how you do it!"

Lazy. Floating, lounging. Barely even talking. Soaking it in. Eventually, even Lori felt the pull of the water. She sat on the edge for a while, twirling her feet in it, until slowly she succumbed. Eased herself in. But only after Buck, who was now lying prostrate in the grass, assured her, "Trust me, your clothes won't stay wet long. Mine are dry already."

Which was true. His cotton T-shirt, mesh basketball shorts, flannel boxers, even his socks and high-tops were dry. The sun wasn't up, and yet the air was pleasantly warm. For some reason, it felt warmer than earlier in the night. Perhaps a hot morning was waiting on the horizon.

Heather had climbed out and gotten dressed and made sure to call everyone else "a buncha prudes" for keeping their clothes on.

"I was naked," Schultz assured her, which was technically true because he had taken his shorts off under the water for a few minutes. "I was right there with you, babe."

"Not that anyone would notice," Jared said.

Even though the barb slid right off Schultz—sitting contentedly in the grass with his arm around Heather—Jared immediately regretted it.

"Sorry," he said. "That was mean."

"But it's true," Schultz said with a shrug. "Wanna see?"

He stood up and put his hands on his waistband.

"Pass," Jared said.

Schultz shrugged again, sat back down. Put his arm back around his girl.

"So, what happens to you two?" Bev asked.

"Us?" Heather replied, placing her head on Schultz's shoulder.

"Yeah," Bev said. "You keeping this thing going in college?"

Both Heather and Schultz were silent. They eyed each other: *You telling them, or am I?*

Heather spoke first. "We'll see what—"

"Happens," Schultz said, then he kissed her on the cheek.

Everyone knew what would happen. Schultz was going to Cornell. Heather was going to Pratt. A few letters, a few calls, perhaps. Maybe they'd hook up over Thanksgiving or Christmas, but that would be the coda to their fling.

"*We've got tonight,*" Schultz sang with a wink.

"*Who needs tomorrow?*" Heather sang back. Louder, and with feeling.

"Go ahead and have your tonight, babes, but I'm goin' home," Lori said as she climbed out of the water.

"Wait, what?" Buck said.

"I don't know what time it is," Lori said. "But I'm bone-tired. And swimming was . . . better than expected. Got me relaxed and ready to go home. I don't want to be too sleepy when I drive."

"You're our ride, though," Buck said. "I think me and Heather wanna stay a bit."

Heather nodded enthusiastically and then snuggled in closer to Schultz.

"Ride with us," Schultz said. "I mean, if that's cool with Bev."

Bev, still in the water, spit a stream from her mouth—an arcing fountain—and shrugged a *sure, whatever.*

Trevor wasn't about to offer up Sarah's car as a second option, but he turned to her to see if she might. She took it the wrong way, assuming he was ready to leave too.

"Don't you dare go with Lori," she said to him.

The truth was that the thought hadn't crossed his mind until that moment. But now that the option was on the table, he considered it. A ride home with Lori would be awkward— he hardly knew her—but it meant he'd arrive home to a soft bed and some time alone to contemplate the evening. This was what he had wanted earlier.

Not anymore. The water had seemed to satisfy Lori enough that she was ready to leave. It did something else for him. It left him wanting. It found him yearning.

"Don't worry," he told Sarah. "I'm staying."

It's becoming clear to me that this world is different. It's the little things that give it away. The signs. The cars. The clothes. The shape of the lights.

It feels older. Yet newer. A past friendship rekindled, but not the same.

I'm not sure I belong here. But I know for sure I don't belong there either.

I push forward through the predawn light.

Cure for Pain

Lori went the wrong way.

At least that's how it looked to Trevor. She paced around the pool to the side opposite from where everyone came in, and she headed toward the woods.

"The trail is over here!" Trevor shouted, pointing back over his shoulder.

"No, it isn't," Lori called back. "I see it clearly. Right in front of me."

She skipped happily, which seemed uncharacteristic. But what did Trevor know? His experiences with Lori amounted to a couple of classes and the occasional party. Dour and depressed? Yes. But perhaps only some of the time. Because people contained multitudes, didn't they? At least that's what the poets said.

"That must be a different trail," Sarah told her. "Because Trevor is right. It's back the other way."

The place had symmetry. The pool, ensconced in darkness, may have appeared nearly identical along its opposite sides. But Trevor and Sarah had watched the others arrive. They were almost entirely certain about which end was which.

Lori wasn't listening, though. She simply tossed a dismissive hand their way, spun on a heel, and slipped into the darkness as if it were a robe after a shower. Her exit was accompanied by a sound—a gentle puff, an exhalation from the forest. Not frightening, but odd nonetheless.

"We should go after her," Sarah said. "She's definitely going the wrong way."

"But where did she go?" Trevor asked. "I circled this place. I didn't see another trail anywhere."

"She wouldn't just wander off into the woods," Heather said.

"Really?" Jared replied. "We're talking about Lori, aren't we?"

"What's that supposed to mean?" Heather said.

Everyone knew what that was supposed to mean. Rumors about Lori abounded. About the scars on her thighs. About her three-night hospital stay six months earlier and how it wasn't due to appendicitis like her parents claimed. Heather was her best friend, and she knew more about Lori than most. But she clearly didn't know everything. And that must have worried her.

"I'll find her," Heather said, since no one else was willing to make an effort.

Then she was on her feet. So was Schultz. They followed Lori's path until they reached the edge of the woods. They searched. Crouched. Peered. Didn't step into the darkness. Instead, Schultz picked up a stick and began poking at the trees.

"They won't bite," Buck called out.

"There's no trail," Schultz called back. "At least not one I can see. The growth seems pretty thick. Pure black out there."

Hands clasped and held near her chin, Heather paced back and forth by the edge of the woods. "What the fuck, what the fuck," she murmured. And then she yelled, "Lori! Lori! Come back!"

No answer.

"There's definitely no trail?" Jared asked.

Frustrated, Schultz threw his stick into the darkness. "Nothing even close."

"Maybe we shouldn't worry," Trevor said. "I mean, she seemed kinda okay to me. Happy even."

This was clear. Her dip in the pool had done something to her. Something good. So why question it?

"I'm going after her," Heather said.

"Then I'm coming with you," Schultz said. "Anyone pack a machete?"

The spot where they stepped into the forest may have been the same spot that Lori did. If it wasn't, then it was close. The darkness wrapped itself around them too, but there was no sound when they left. Not that there should've been. Still, it was a clear difference.

The others waited, watched the spot like it was an egg ripe with a baby bird. Ready for a crack. An emergence. Joy and relief.

None came. Time passed. How much? It wasn't clear. Trevor couldn't stand it anymore. He broke the silence.

"What's happening out there?" he called.

No answer.

So he stood. But rather than follow them, he headed in the other direction.

"Where are you going?" Sarah asked.

"Back to the main trail," Trevor said. "We were in such a rush to get here, maybe we missed some other trails that forked off from it. Maybe that's where they ended up."

It was a reasonable assumption. Though he thought it was also possible that there was a different parking spot somewhere, and perhaps other trails that led to that. Grabbing Sarah's Maglite off the ground, he searched the woods on the other side of the pool.

In childhood games of flashlight tag, of manhunter, of ghost in the graveyard, the danger was the thrill. The darkness was the point. But now . . .

"I can't see anything," Trevor said. "The light doesn't seem to go anywhere."

"Go farther down the trail, then," Sarah said.

"I can't see the trail."

"How can you not see the trail?" Jared said. "It's not like the night could've gotten any darker."

Trevor wasn't lying. He walked up and down the periphery of the woods with the Maglite, but the beam couldn't penetrate the wall of dark. And there was no trail. Not anymore.

"Maybe I *am* on the wrong side," Trevor said, even though he was sure his mind couldn't be playing such fiendish tricks. Still, he hurried to the area where the others had disappeared from. Scanned it with the Maglite. No trail there either. Nowhere for the light to even go.

"Can you stop fucking around?" Bev said. "Find them already."

"I'm telling you there are no trails anywhere," Trevor said.

"I may be high," Buck said. "But I'm not high enough to believe that shit. Gimme the light."

Then Buck walked the same circuit. Checked the same spots. Did the identical things. Only with a puffed-up chest and slower gait. His verdict?

"What the hell?"

"I know," Trevor said. "It doesn't make any sense."

"This is one of those TV-remote-is-in-the-couch-cushions-the-whole-time situations, isn't it?" Sarah said.

Unsurprisingly, it became her turn with the Maglite. She did a pass too. Paced, searched. Slow and meticulous. With each step and each thrust of the beam into the black, her shoulders sagged. Her confidence waned. Until . . .

"Jesus," she said, and she placed the light down.

"Okay," Jared said. "You're all messing with me, right? The situation is not that dire, is it?"

"You can check too if you want," Sarah said with a sigh. "But there are no trails, no obvious places to go anywhere. Pure black beyond the first row of trees. That's it."

She sat. Legs splayed. She tore grass from the ground and threw the tiny bits of sod to the side. Trevor wanted to comfort her, but how could he? None of this made any sense.

"Should I go after them too?" Buck asked. "I feel like I should go after them."

"I'll come with you," Trevor said.

"No one is going anywhere," Sarah said.

"Don't worry about that with me," Jared said, still navel

deep in the shallow end of the pool. "I'm not moving an inch from this spot."

Buck moved. He paced with purpose.

"I said don't go in there," Sarah commanded.

"Chill out," he said. "I just need to smoke."

When he reached his backpack, he crouched down. Fiddled with the stubborn zipper until he had an opening big enough to shove a hand inside. It emerged with a ziplock bag containing his stash and paraphernalia.

He packed a bowl with the efficiency of an assembly-line worker and sparked it up with a Zippo. After a very long pull, he said, "Welcome to join me," before exhaling a tsunami of skunky smoke.

"I'm not sure that's the best idea," Trevor said. "What if one of them is hurt?"

"All the more reason to get toasted," Buck said. "Don't want to face any gory shit without some herbal spectacles."

"Yeah," Trevor said. "But one of us might have to drive. Like . . . to the hospital."

"Won't be me," Sarah said as she hopped up and then over to Buck's side. "I'll take some."

It was obvious what Sarah was doing. Drinking, smoking, it was all a scheme to lock herself into this spot for the night. Trevor would never support her driving drunk or stoned. If he wanted to go home with her, he was going to have to wait things out.

While Sarah didn't smoke very often, she wasn't a novice. Still, she wasn't experienced enough with weed to avoid coughing. It started through her nose, smoke jetting out like pistons from her nostrils. Soon she was doubled over and hacking, her eyes watering. Trevor rushed to her side.

"You okay?" he asked.

"Fine," she said with a sniffle. "I've never been . . . good at that."

Buck presented the bowl to Bev. She stared at it for a moment, then turned to Jared. He waved her off.

"None for me, thank you," Jared said.

"I know that, but what about me? Will you drive my car?" Bev asked him.

"Of course, but I'm not ready to leave yet," Jared said.

"Neither am I," Bev said. "I just feel like I need something to calm me down. I'm a little freaked out right now."

She didn't wait for Jared to respond. She simply snagged the bowl. Though not as seasoned as Buck, she handled her hit with aplomb. Blew a couple smoke rings for good measure. The bowl ended up back with Buck, and after another relaxed toke, he held it out to Trevor like he was handing him some hallowed sword. Or that's how it felt to Trevor. He was the definition of inexperienced when it came to weed. One hit off one joint at one party one time. That was it. Didn't even inhale, as they say.

But now? Now he wanted to be without worry and entirely with Sarah. In mind and body. Would weed give him that? Maybe not, but . . .

"Okay," he said as he grabbed it. "Remind me what to do."

                              *   *   *

They lost time. At least Trevor did. Two hits and his own fit of
coughing later, and his eyes locked into the reflection of the
tiki torches on the water. Like watching the clouds, he picked
out shapes. Animals and objects, sure. But also memories.
Ideas. Emotions. Circling back on one another and leaving him
unbound to even the concept of seconds or minutes or hours.

It was enough to make him want to close his eyes. When
he did, his mind traveled to the future. College. A dorm room
with white brick walls and a view onto the quad. Frisbee. A
lecture class with a teacher sitting cross-legged on a desk and
opining on the Civil Rights Movement. Autumn leaves on the
ground, the perfect mix of red, yellow, and orange. A frat party
with a Slip 'n Slide in the yard. Bright green Jell-O shots. A late
night in the library, sitting down and leaning against the
stacks, dozing off. Papers. Oral presentations. Tests, tests, and
more tests. Finally, a sunny day, a dignified celebrity giving a
speech, and caps thrown skyward. After that? A return home
to lay down roots in the new development off Sudbury. A good
job and a good car with a multidisk changer. A girlfriend who
would soon be a wife, but for now was someone who liked to
eat out at restaurants with Tuscan chicken on the menu and go
to college basketball games with a painted face and lace up
tall boots for Sunday hikes. Was it Sarah? If not, she sure
looked like her.

None of this comforted Trevor, exactly. It also didn't scare him. It was like he was at an open house, walking through the rooms of a possible future. He was under no obligation to buy. Simply having a look. Though it seemed like the type of future he would buy. Scratch that. *Should* buy. The reward for all his hard work. And, curiously enough, it was the only future he had time to envision. Because he was interrupted. They all were. By a voice.

Heather.

"Oh, thank god," she said as she and Schultz stepped out of the darkness on the opposite side of the pool from where they entered.

Buck, who'd been lying down, popped up like a sprung trap. "Did you find Lori?"

"I don't think so?" Schultz said, panting.

"What does that mean?" Sarah asked.

"It's . . . strange out there," Heather said softly.

"How long were we gone?" Schultz asked.

Trevor would have guessed hours. But Buck said, "A few minutes, maybe."

"It felt like . . . I don't know what it felt like," Heather said. "It felt different."

The fear in her voice was a virus, escaping from her body and searching for a host.

"You're freaking us out right now," Bev said. "Just tell us if you saw Lori."

"Pretty sure she's gone, or else we would've run into her," Schultz said.

"It felt like we were in the forest for ages," Heather said.

"Or for no time at all," Schultz said between breaths. "I need to sit."

"Me too," Heather said.

Hunched over, Schultz plodded toward them, but when he spied the water, his posture stiffened. "Actually, I need to swim."

Heather turned to the pool as well and the same thing happened to her body. "Yeah," she said. "Swimming might help."

No one questioned it. They simply watched as the two, still fully dressed, waded into the shallow end until the water was up to their ribs and then they fell backward into it, sending out waves that lapped against the pool's edges. It was a baptism of sorts. Because when they emerged, their mood was entirely different. They were radiant.

"Oh my god, I feel so much better," Heather said, pushing wet hair away from her face.

"Thank you, thank you, thank you," Schultz said as he rubbed his eyes.

Trevor's paranoia and euphoria jostled for supremacy. And in the space between the two, he had a moment of clarity. It echoed through the rest of the group in the form of questions.

"What's happening right now?" Bev asked.

"Yeah," Jared said. "This doesn't feel right, does it?"

"Why won't you tell us what the hell was out there?" Buck asked.

Heather looked conspiratorially at Schultz and asked, "Could you describe it?"

He took a moment. Then sighed and said, "Not in words exactly. But it felt . . . lost? Not in a terrible way. But not in a good way."

"Fuck it," Buck said. "I'm seeing for myself."

Before anyone could stop him, Buck was on his feet and heading for the darkness. Only there was no way to know for sure if he was entering at the same place that the others did.

"Should he be going out there?" Jared asked Heather and Schultz.

"If he wants to go, I guess he should go," Heather said.

"I don't necessarily think it's dangerous," Schultz said.

"Do you know what you're doing, Buck?" Bev shouted as he reached the edge of the forest.

Buck's arm shot skyward, and he flashed her a thumbs-up. "I'm setting everyone's heads back on straight. Some of y'all can't handle your booze or your weed. That's for sure."

Revving up his engine like a cartoon character, he ran in place, kicking up dirt and twigs. Then he lowered a shoulder and plowed into the darkness.

Silence. And waiting. Tension, pudding thick.

"I need to get back in the water too," Jared said, and he joined Heather and Schultz, entering at the shallow end, dunking under and then gliding past them.

Bev wasn't far behind.

Sarah didn't join them. Instead, she paced toward where Buck had entered the darkness, stopping at least ten yards from the edge. Trevor followed her at a short distance because he wanted to stop her if she decided to launch her own investigation. Thankfully, she sat down. Cross-legged, she stared at the darkness.

"He's probably right," she said. "It's super late. Some of us have had a lot to drink. And smoke. Buck is used to it, though. He can handle it."

"I'm not sure that I can," Buck said with a sigh.

He was back, only he had returned at the opposite end of the pool and had now snuck up behind them. It didn't make sense. He'd been gone for maybe a minute or two. Probably not even that. To cover that amount of ground, he would've needed to be running fast. And Buck never ran fast. He certainly wasn't out of breath.

"You're okay!" Bev cheered.

"Did you see what we meant?" Heather asked.

Buck nodded robotically, then made a beeline for the pool. He entered from the side, first sitting on the edge, and then rolling his doughy body into the water. Seconds later, he was back at the surface, refreshed.

"Hot damn," he said, slapping himself lightly on the face.

"So can you describe what you saw?" Jared asked.

Buck shook his head. "All I can say is *this right here* . . . ? This is the place to be."

I need a rest, so I take a detour through the brambles and wet ferns.

When I get to the spot where we were supposed to go, I sit on a rock and watch the sun rise.

I smell the dewy grass and the greedy weeds, and I look down on the houses I know and the ones I don't, and I try to figure out my place in this place.

I want to scream. Instead, I cry. For as long and hard as I've ever cried. It feels terrible and necessary.

I know I haven't made a mistake. Still. Something's not right about this. That's becoming obvious, even though I need to see more.

When I get back through the field, I turn toward town.

Fade Into You

They didn't speak to each other for a while.
Sarah took to the water. Trevor did too, and as soon as he was immersed, the weed loosened its grip on him. He wasn't lost in his thoughts anymore. Only in the moment. And the moment seemed to stretch on and on.

Sarah pulled herself out of the water at one point and marched around the edge of woods. This time she wasn't searching for an escape route. It looked more like standing guard. Protecting the oasis.

"I'm not the least bit worried about Lori," she stated. "I think she found her happiness and her way home. But I'm not ready to leave yet. I say we wait until the sun comes up."

They were all cool with that. Buck packed another bowl, and Schultz and Heather joined him in a smoky session. Bev cracked open another Boone's, which was passed around and consumed straight from the bottle.

Then they split off into factions:

Buck, Heather, and Schultz, at the edge of the pool with feet swirling the water, dropping leaves onto the surface and tracking their slow voyages out into the middle.

Jared and Bev on a bench, their heads resting against each other, with a folded sweatshirt acting as a keystone.

Sarah and Trevor in the grass, near the spring, where the bubbling sounds kept their conversation private.

"So, what do you think?" Sarah asked.

"About staying until sunrise?" Trevor said.

"About all of it. This place. This moment."

A hard question to answer. It felt like they were trapped, locked in by the darkness. Yet that didn't worry him. What happened to Lori didn't worry him either. He wondered if that made him a cold person. Though he was certain he wasn't a cold person.

"I didn't imagine the night would go this way, that's for sure," he said.

Sarah laughed.

"Did you?" he asked.

"Of course not, but I'm not mad about it."

They were sitting cross-legged, facing each other. She reached forward. Cold hands on his bare knees. He shivered. And smiled. It felt like a game of chicken. Who would pull away first?

Neither.

"Let me tell you how tonight was *supposed* to go," she said. "You know, before you let the cat out of the bag. We were gonna finish our quest. Like the rock stars we are. Sliding in and sliding out. Even the Purple Lady never would've heard us. Unfortunately, that would've meant we'd never know about this place. But we would've completed the others. Checked every box on our map."

She gave his knees a squeeze.

"Do you know about the lookout on Hupper Hill?" she asked. "With the rock wall? Along the cliff's edge?"

"I wanna say . . . maybe?"

"Well, you *were* gonna know about it, because I was gonna take you there," she told him. "It's not far from here, actually, but it isn't easy to find. It's near where the water tower used to be. Remember? The one with all the graffiti?"

"They tore it down when we were in, like, second grade?"

"Sounds right," Sarah said. "Hupper Hill is behind where it was, just past the field and through the brush, an absolutely stunning vista. Once you get there, you can see all of Sutton. It's like in those movies when people are in Los Angeles and they're up by the Hollywood sign or whatever. Nothing but sky. Trees. Twinkling lights. Pools."

"Pools!"

"Our conquered kingdom, Trevor," she said, and she squeezed harder. "We would have seen it all."

"So, what would've happened next?" he asked.

"I would've told you to cancel that stupid camping trip," Sarah said. "I would've let you know that Mike and I are officially over, and how that's a good thing. I would've explained that . . ."

She paused. And he held his breath. To say Trevor had been waiting for this particular bit of information was an understatement. He'd harbored countless fantasies about the demise of that relationship. One scenario involved Mike showing up at his door and trying to punch Trevor out. Trevor would be too quick, catching Mike's fist in the air with one hand, while wagging a finger with the other. The jilted young man would concede a bloodless defeat and skulk away, never to be seen again. Ridiculous? Undoubtedly. But so was what Sarah told him next.

"I would've explained that I've been practicing making paper airplanes."

"Okay," he said. "Not what I expected."

"It's relevant. I've been practicing making paper airplanes because I was gonna make one out of that map. That map has been through a lot, but I'm confident that with my tight folds, I could've made it into a big ol' jet airliner."

Trevor resisted the urge to finish the Steve Miller lyric, mostly because he wanted to see where this strange tangent was heading.

"Go on."

"Well," she said. "I was gonna throw that plane over the edge, let it fly down toward Sutton, swooping and gliding and escaping from us."

Her hands let go of his knees and her arms spread like wings. She swayed. Leaned forward, and then back. Breathed in through her nose to fill her engine.

"What else?" he asked.

"I was gonna watch you," she said. "I was gonna watch you watch it."

He wasn't sure if he should be flattered or freaked out. He chose the former.

"Huh," he said. "That's . . . nice."

"I hoped it would be," she replied. "And if watching our little map plane made you happy, I was gonna kiss you."

"You . . . ?"

"And if watching it made you sad, I was also gonna kiss you. And if you didn't watch it at all, and if you chose instead to watch me watching you, well . . . I was gonna kiss you."

"Really?"

"Really. And I still—"

He kissed her.

A little more than a peck, but not all in. Pulling back, he checked her eyes. They were closed, so he closed his. Then this time, *she* leaned in. Their noses grazed against each other until they found an angle to nestle. They fell into a longer kiss, a deeper kiss, a kiss he had hoped would come, though he had never imagined it would come this way, in this place, surrounded by these people. Of course, he didn't think about any of that now. Instead, his mind lingered on the rough-smooth texture of her lips on his. The soft of her cheek. The tickling play of her hair. The sound of the spring, like bubbles popping on the surface of a simmer.

"I like this," she whispered, after stopping for a breath, and a giggle.

"Uh-huh," Trevor said, and he leaned in for more.

It was like swimming. Weightless and free. A feeling of never wanting it to end. It was like all the kisses Trevor had experienced, but also none of them. Because he had never felt about someone the way he felt about Sarah.

Trevor's first kiss, or at least the one he counted as first, was in seventh grade. A school dance. Dim lighting and streamers. An emergency exit near the back of the gymnasium that didn't sound an alarm when opened. It had been tested many times, and when Trevor shouldered it open, the tests had proven true. He slipped quietly outside.

Gina Barnes had told him to meet Bonnie Silverstein next to the spot where the janitor parked his van. It was dark there, and Bonnie had a surprise for him. The surprise was the kiss. Teeth and tongue and the taste of Binaca spray. It was exciting and not-at-all-terrible for a first time, but it was the only kiss with Bonnie. They "dated" for a week, but that mostly meant smiling at each other in the hall. Then it was April break, and when they got back to school, Bonnie told him that she needed some time alone. They still smiled at each other in the hall, only not as widely. Trevor was more confused than hurt. Though when he found out that Paul Tillet had played Seven Minutes in Heaven with Bonnie at Jessica Kim's birthday party, things made a bit more sense. Most girls ended up kissing Paul Tillet at some point.

His second kiss was with Maria Bartolo. Ninth grade. During soccer tryouts. Boys' and girls' teams held them during the last two weeks of August at the fields by the fire station. A neighborhood carpool led to Trevor and Maria sitting in the back seat of Maria's older sister's Dodge Dart. Sweaty, slightly stinky, but not in an awful way, they bonded over a disdain for wind sprints and the Coerver Method. By the end of the week, they were holding hands in the back seat and talking on the phone for two hours a night.

The kiss came in an empty playground. They met there on a Sunday evening, and sat together at a picnic table, where they shared a milkshake Maria had made at home in her blender. So their mouths were cold when they kissed, a more pleasant sensation than Trevor had anticipated.

Over the next few weeks, there was more kissing and awkward explorations, but never beneath clothes. Then the relationship puttered to a stop, near the end of soccer season. They realized that soccer was the main thing they talked about. And while Maria was a rising star and already on varsity, Trevor was an average JV player. It was another amicable split.

No kisses and no girlfriends sophomore year. Followed by a junior year where Trevor got drunk for the second time in his life, at a New Year's Eve party where a sloppy make-out session on a basement couch with his friend Rachel Dunbar led to the proverbial second and third bases. It was wonderful and embarrassing in equal measure, and both he and Rachel seemed to regret it. It was months before they could talk to each other without blushing.

At the end of junior year, he started dating Kelly Lake, and the first kiss with her came after their first date: a dinner at Bennigan's and a screening of *Cliffhanger*. They kissed in her car in the parking lot, and both had enough experience that it felt natural. It also felt natural when they slept together three months later. In August, in her room, while her parents were away at their camp in the Finger Lakes. It was as hot as August gets, and all they had was an oscillating fan to keep them cool. They were fine with it.

It wasn't Kelly's first time. She'd had a serious boyfriend before and was already on the pill. But she wasn't exactly seasoned. It was experimental for both, and they were fastidious about condoms and communication. It was as responsible and respectful as such things could be.

Neither of them was entirely at fault for the end of the relationship. Jealousies on both sides cropped up. Kelly had a group of three guy friends that she had been close with since eighth grade, when she went to Saint Vincent's, a Catholic school a few towns over. The guys went to a different high school, so naturally Trevor couldn't trust them. Especially whenever Kelly would mention hanging out with one of them in some town that might as well have been on another planet. Similarly, Kelly wasn't thrilled about the time Trevor spent with certain girls working late into the evening on the school paper. Even though Trevor assured her that he wasn't interested in his coworkers like that.

It all ended at a Halloween party, where they both showed up separately: Kelly dressed as a cat, and Trevor as Waldo from the Where's Waldo? books. Trevor's jealousies boiled over when he saw that Kelly had arrived with one of those aforementioned alien boys from eighth grade, who was dressed like a character from A *Clockwork Orange*—never a good sign. So Trevor drank too much and danced with Rachel Dunbar, who was dressed as Wonder Woman and also drank too much. What happened before happened again. Waldo and Wonder Woman kissed. It wasn't much more than a peck, but the cat saw it, so the cat ran off with the guy in the black bowler hat and white codpiece. The relationship ended that night.

A few weeks later, Trevor started hanging out with Sarah. It started, funnily enough, with the school paper. Trevor was one of the editors, and Sarah submitted an op-ed about how school lunches should be free. Titled "So Long and Thanks for All the Fish Sticks," it was simultaneously hilarious and empathetic, and it charmed Trevor to no end. He did have a few notes, however. Sarah was impressed by how smart and thorough the notes were, working to strengthen her argument rather than scold her about grammar and word count. The mutual admiration society began, and they fell quickly and easily into a friendship. While there was nothing exclusive about the relationship—Sarah was tangled up with Mike— Trevor kept himself single and available for the rest of the year. On a dream, on a hunch, on a hope . . .

"Oh baby, oh baby . . . oh baby!"

Buck's voice was unmistakable, and unmistakably loud, and it cracked the shell of Trevor and Sarah's moment. When Trevor turned to look in Buck's direction, he was greeted with a crude but amusing gesture: Buck humping one of the log benches.

Bev slapped him on the back. Hard. "Don't be an ass."

"I'm only looking at the boy–girl ratio," Buck told her. "And I'm thinking this is the best shot I have."

A fair point. There were Trevor and Sarah. Schultz and Heather. Jared and Bev. And there was Buck. The odd man out.

Jared and Bev weren't exactly a perfect match. They were good friends, sure, but no one would ever expect it to be more than that. Bev and Buck, however, seemed even less compatible. They were always cordial to each other, but Bev had confessed to Sarah that she often found Buck's party-all-the-time persona annoying. The feeling was probably mutual. Trevor had learned that Buck, Heather, and Lori had a private nickname for Bev: Ringwald. On account of her resemblance to the actress and the characters she played, which they viewed as boy-crazy goody-goodies. Not entirely fair. To Bev or Ringwald. And certainly not a term of endearment.

"I'm just glad you two have finally made it public," Schultz said.

"What?" Trevor said. "There was nothing to make public."

"Pfff," Heather said. "Come on. That wasn't the first time you kissed her."

Sarah shrugged: *Whaddya gonna do?*

Trevor shrugged as well: *It ain't for lack of trying.*

"You two!" Schultz cried. "What the hell have you been up to all this time?"

"Swimming," Sarah said plainly.

They kept swimming. Like walking past a bowl of candy on the counter, the draw was irresistible. All seven of them were compelled to dip in. To dive under. To float on top. To savor again and again.

"You ever see one of those old musicals?" Jared asked. "Where women in swim caps create designs by, like . . . swim-dancing?"

"I don't watch anything in black and white," Buck said. "That shit is boring."

"I've seen the *SNL* skit with Martin Short," Heather said. "Synchronized swimming. That shit is hilarious."

The conversation slid into discussions of *Saturday Night Live* and which season and which performers were the best. Trevor zoned out, floated on his back for a while, eyes closed. Until *tap, tap, tap* on his forehead.

He opened his eyes, expecting to see Sarah. Bev was treading water there instead.

"Hey, guy," she whispered.

Trevor had floated away from the crowd, into the shallow end, and there was no one within at least sixty feet of them. So, Bev had obviously abandoned the chat and sought him out.

He wiped the water from his face and asked, "What's up?"

He expected her to press him for details on the kiss, or perhaps she was trying to ferret out his intentions about Sarah. They were best friends after all. But instead, she told him, "I trust you because you've kept my secret."

"Your . . . ?"

"About my mom. I appreciate that. And your mom has been a big help too."

It had been a while since Trevor had thought about Bev's mom, and that worried him. Because he knew that she was probably thinking about her all the time.

"How's she doing?" he asked.

She shrugged. "The chemo is gonna be rough, but what can you do? Not like there are other options. She doesn't go for that New Agey stuff."

"Maybe she could—"

"I don't want to talk about my mom right now," Bev said. "Or not directly. I want to talk about something else. You're a level-headed guy. You don't ignore the rules."

"Is that a compliment?"

"In this case, yes. Because I need someone who respects the space-time continuum."

"A good thing to respect."

"Can you be quiet for a moment?" she asked.

"Like right—"

She reached forward with pinched fingers and zipped his lip. Then she patted him on the cheek. It did the trick. They were left with the sounds of the water lapping against the edge of the pool and the faraway drone of the others acting out their favorite late-night sketches. Until—

SHI-WOOOO

"There," she said. "Did you hear that?"

He nodded because he wasn't sure if he was supposed to

remain silent. Also, because he did hear it: a sound like an owl or a woodwind. Though it was neither of those things. It was alive but hollow. Natural and melodious. Familiar, and yet not entirely.

"Okay," Bev said. "Now start counting to yourself and stop counting when you hear it again."

Bev closed her eyes, and her lips started moving—*one, two, three*—and Trevor mimicked, though he added *Mississippis* to the mix.

Four Mississippi, five Mississippi, six Mississippi . . . all the way up to one hundred sixteen Mississippi, when—

SHI-WOOOO

"There," Bev said. "You heard it again, didn't you?"

He nodded. A lovely sound.

"It's okay," Bev said. "You can talk now."

"What was it?" he asked. "An animal?"

"I don't know, but it happens every two minutes or so. Without fail."

"Really?"

"I've done the count dozens of times," she said. "It's always the same."

Given the odd feelings this place seemed to inspire in Trevor, he wasn't about to question anyone's motives, but he asked, "Is counting something that helps you?"

She shrugged and said, "I have insomnia. Or I've had it recently. You know, with everything going on in my family. I got rid of the clock in my room because I thought that would help, but I've become obsessed with counting. We have a cuckoo clock downstairs, and my dad took out the cuckoo sounds because it was annoying. But it still runs, and up in my room, at night, when it's quiet, I can still hear the gears and the hands, and I can count out time by waiting to hear certain clicks."

"I'm not sure what you're telling me. Are you worried about falling asleep? You could go home. You could—"

"We've been here for at least two days," she said plainly.

"What?"

"Every time I hear that sound, I count it in my head. And every time I count it thirty times, it means at least an hour has passed, and I make a mark in the dirt over there." She pointed to a spot near where the water poured in from the spring.

Not that he didn't trust her, but Trevor wanted to see, so he sidestroked over and stopped along the edge. Sure enough, there were tally marks scratched on the ground, like evidence of a schoolyard game.

"Fifty hours," Bev said. That was also what the marks seemed to indicate, though it seemed impossible.

SHI-WOOOO

Trevor hadn't been counting, but it did feel like two minutes had passed. Had Bev really counted over a thousand of these? Thinking back, he did remember seeing her carrying a stick, and walking over to this edge of the pool, multiple times. He assumed she was trying to find somewhere inconspicuous to take a bathroom break.

Speaking of . . . How many times had he peed? Had he peed at all? He couldn't remember. Could it be possible that two days had passed and he hadn't even peed?

"No," he finally said. "That's not right. The sun hasn't come up."

"And the stars haven't come out," Bev said. "And have you noticed the snacks? And the Boone's?"

"What about them?"

"They haven't run out," she said. "They're always full."

This also didn't make sense, but when Trevor turned to the benches where they had left the drinks, there was indeed a rainbow of bottles.

"Am I still . . . ? Is the weed . . . ?"

Bev shook her head, but she didn't have to. The effects of the weed had worn off long ago. It wasn't his head that was the problem. It was this place.

"First there was the whole thing with Lori. And now there's this. We should tell the others, right?" Bev said.

"Have you already told Sarah?"

Bev shook her head. "She wouldn't care. She likes it here. She doesn't want an excuse to leave."

"Should you and I go . . . out there?" He motioned with his chin to the darkness.

It didn't frighten him as much as it worried him, because he wasn't sure what exactly he wanted. To step into that dark forest would confirm one of two things. Either there was something askew here, or this was all in his head and he could walk away like Lori did.

To say something was askew didn't mean it was wrong. It was like having an uncomfortable dream, then becoming aware that it was a dream, but not waking up. Which meant

115

he could possibly take the reins, steer the narrative to its ideal conclusion. Entering the woods, however, had changed Schultz, Heather, and Buck. They appeared more at peace with their situation. Or perhaps more oblivious. If he stepped out there, would he lose control of the dream? Or would he wake up?

"I wouldn't go out there," Bev said.

"Go where?" a voice asked.

It was Jared, who had quietly swum over.

"Hey, you," Bev said, and she put an arm around him.

"Where are you going?" he asked. "Out into the woods?"

"I was thinking about it," Trevor said.

"It isn't worth it," Jared said. "Look at the three of them over there. They went out in those woods, and now they're hanging around doing *Wayne's World* impressions and acting like this isn't totally weird."

"Right?" Bev said. "It is weird, isn't it?"

"Sarah didn't go into the woods," Trevor reminded them.

"Sarah's always out in the woods," Jared said, but then he provided an addendum. "Which is a compliment. She's an explorer."

"I love her to death, but yeah, that girl doesn't need any encouragement to get lost," Bev said.

"How long do you think we've been here?" Trevor asked Jared.

The question made Jared wince. Like an old memory he wanted to forget. "Longer than I think is possible," he said. "Doesn't it seem like the sun should've come up by now?"

"Twice," Bev said. "Should've come up, gone down, and come up again."

"Are you messing with me?" Jared asked.

She shook her head gravely.

"Have we slept?" Trevor asked. "I don't feel tired, so I feel like we might have."

"I honestly don't remember," Jared said.

"This should freak me out," Bev said. "But I don't feel freaked out."

Trevor had to agree. He was as calm as the water around them, and these revelations were simply ripples. Nowhere close to waves.

"If there was a monster and it started chasing you, you would run away, right?" he asked the other two.

"You think there's a monster in the woods?" Jared said.

"No," Trevor said. "It's just an example. If a monster came out of nowhere and started chasing you, you wouldn't stand still because you don't believe in monsters. You would instantly start believing in monsters, and you would run."

"I might wonder if it was someone in a monster suit," Bev said.

"So, what's the monster suit right now?" Trevor asked. "What's preventing you from believing?"

"Believing what?" Jared asked hesitantly.

"That this place is magic."

I stop in the only place that's open. A bagel shop in the spot where the movie theater is supposed to be. I have no money, so I linger near the entrance, pick up the *Sutton Journal* off a high-top table and peruse it.

I see the date. I don't want to believe it, but I think I have to believe it.

I see a name. I definitely don't want to believe it.

It's too much to handle. I sit down.

"Can I help you?" a girl behind the counter asks.

I recognize the distinct spelling on her name tag: Pyper. The only person I know with that spelling is a toddler. This girl is probably older than me. Two Pypers in the same town? What are the odds?

"Pyper Gleason?" I ask.

"Yeah?" she says.

"I just . . . used to know your sister," I say. "Your stepsister, I mean."

"Cool. I haven't talked to her in a few months. She's still out in Portland, though."

I don't respond. The evidence has got me too flustered.
And my instincts are telling me I've got to get the hell
out of here.

I jump up and head for the door.

I Am a Scientist

They assigned jobs. Jared's task was to talk to the others, to suss out their states of mind. Bev focused on devising easier ways to tell time. Trevor's domain was the woods. He wasn't venturing out there, but he would experiment.

The experiments started simply enough, with Trevor throwing things into the darkness. Sticks. Rocks. Chunks of dirt. He'd throw as hard as he could, and he'd listen. Each time he threw something, he didn't hear any breaking or bouncing or ricocheting off trees. Odd.

Remembering how Buck had quickly and incongruously appeared at a different location when he entered the woods, Trevor wondered if the same thing might've happened to the projectiles. But when he surveyed the edges, he found no evidence of reemergence.

Next: the fishing approach. Thin green vines clung to some of the trees that skirted the edge of the darkness and Trevor was able to tear them off. Using skills he'd learned in Boy Scouts, he laced them together until he had a "rope" that was easily thirty feet long. He tied a short, heavy stick to the end. He couldn't swing it and cast it like a lure or grappling hook.

The vine was liable to snap. However, if he kept the line slack, he could still throw the stick and carefully reel it back in.

So that's what he did. He threw the stick and slowly pulled the vine. It came back without resistance. No snags, no bumps, not even signs of dirt on it. Which was certainly strange, because when he repeated the experiment in the torchlit areas around the pool, the stick almost always got caught on twigs, or crashed against rocks, or trolled the ground and carried back clumps of grass or leaves.

As far as Trevor could tell, there was a void past the wall of darkness, or something similarly indescribable, because the ones who went out there certainly couldn't put words to it. Had it tricked their eyes or minds? He wasn't sure, and as much as he wanted to investigate in person, he knew that wasn't wise.

Meanwhile, Bev made a clock. A clever one. The bottles of Boone's were the key. She took a bottle, poured it out, poked a small hole in the cap with her keys, and put the cap back on. Then she poked a small hole in the cap of a full bottle and attached the two bottles together at the caps using medical tape from a first aid kit she kept in her purse.

She had created something akin to an hourglass, though it took far more than an hour for the liquid to pass from one bottle to the other. It was a slow drip. Using that reliable SHI-WOOOO sound as a timer, Bev measured how much liquid collected in twenty minutes and calculated that the top bottle would fill the bottom bottle every six hours. Barring any unseen manipulations.

Flip it four times, and it would measure out a day. Not that she planned to stay any longer than that, but it was a good visual aid to show Trevor. She explained the process, and it seemed logical and helpful, though he wasn't sure if the others would agree.

The others were, in a word, "chill." Jared had asked them how they were feeling, and they had no complaints. He asked them what time they thought it was.

"Late," Buck said.

"The time of our lives," Schultz said.

Finally, he asked them if they wanted to go home.

"Why would you want to abandon a night like this?" Sarah said. "We'll wait until the sun comes up."

Jared reported the conversations back to Trevor and Bev.

"Do you think it's possible that Sarah knows how long we've been here?" Bev asked Trevor.

It wasn't just possible. It was likely. Sarah's awareness of situations was keener than everyone else's. While she didn't much mind the dangers of embarrassment or trespassing offenses, she took the safety of her friends seriously. "Better off at home than in the morning paper," she had told Bev on more than one occasion when a party was getting out of hand or a boy's intentions were inching toward the dangerous. Like a mother hen, she was always on alert.

She clearly must've known something was off here. So she must've trusted it was an acceptable risk. Why, though? Only one way to know.

"Can we talk?" Trevor asked her.

"Oh, is it over already? Summer lovin', had us a blast?" Clearly, she was joking. Mostly.

"Of course it's not over. It's about something else."

He walked her away from Buck, Schultz, and Heather. He showed her the stick and the vines. He told her about the sound and demonstrated the clock. He explained it all, and asked, "Is this something you were wondering about too?"

A thumbnail in her mouth, she appeared a tad guilty. "I've stopped wondering," she said. "I've accepted this place."

"What does that mean?"

"I'm not questioning anything. I'm enjoying this moment for what it is."

"The sun isn't coming up. You're not questioning that? Because that's when you said we'd leave. At sunrise."

"We can't leave."

"Lori left."

"But she didn't want to be here. Don't you want to be here? With me?"

The answer was a resounding yes. Yet he still said, "I want to know *how* to leave."

Sarah gave him a pat on the butt. Loving. But also condescending. "You could spend all your time doing that. Or you could simply enjoy yourself."

Trevor wasn't feeling particularly tense, but he still wanted to know how to get back on that trail to the car. Lori figured it out. As did somebody else.

"What did he say to you?" Trevor asked.

"Who?"

"That guy. The one without the shirt who was leaving here when we were arriving. He whispered something to you."

Sarah paused. "He said to have fun."

"That's it?"

"What else would there be?"

If Sarah was lying to him, he couldn't tell.

"What about the Purple Woman?" he asked. "Did she mention anything else about this place?"

"When would I have talked to her?" Sarah said. "Besides, I don't look like a bunch of grapes or lilacs, so she probably hardly noticed me."

It was safe to say that Sarah was starting to annoy him. Still, he pressed on.

"What about Schultz and Heather and Buck?" he asked. "Do they know something is wrong?"

She shrugged.

"We should tell them, shouldn't we?" he said.

She shrugged again.

It was clear that her priorities lay elsewhere. So Trevor took another tack. He left Sarah, rounded up the rest of the troops, and brought them to her. With Bev's "hourglass" and his "fishing line" in hand, he provided the rundown. Fidgeting their hands, Bev and Jared watched. Staring blankly, Schultz, Heather, and Buck listened.

When Trevor was finished, Schultz said, "I heard everything you said. I believe everything you said. And yet I'm not sure I care."

Heather kissed him on the cheek, pledging solidarity. Buck cleared his throat and said, "Lemme tell you something about what it's like out there in the woods. I've been thinking about how to describe it. And all I can say is that it's like another type of swimming. Like being underwater. Peaceful, until it isn't. Until you're, like, scrambling for air. So, you push your way through, and you end up back here. Where you can breathe again. And feel safe."

"But I don't wanna know how to end up back here," Trevor said. "Or in there. I wanna know there's a way to get home."

"If it's not through the woods, then maybe . . ." Bev motioned with her chin to the water.

"What do you mean?" Jared asked.

"Has anyone touched the bottom yet?" Bev asked. "I mean, in the middle of the pool. Not the shallow end or the edges."

"I haven't really tried," Trevor said.

"Who's the best swimmer here?" Bev asked.

It wasn't a question that needed asking. All eyes turned to Heather.

Heather's tale was one of two lives. In elementary and middle school, she was the exemplar of accomplishment, the type of kid who dominated spelling bees, piano recitals, and, most notably, swim meets. She still held several records at the local Y.

High school changed her. Quite literally. Freshman year, while lacing up her sneakers in the gym, a loose fluorescent bulb fell from a fixture and onto her head. It didn't really hurt her physically. But she stayed home from the school the next day, and the day after that, and the day after that, and . . .

Three weeks in total. When she returned, she hadn't changed radically. She was still talented. But her motivation was replaced by a drier sense of humor, a giddy *fuck-it-all* attitude that's often typical of teenagers.

"Just call me Sir Isaac Edison," she told people. It was a nerd joke, a portmanteau of Sir Isaac Newton and Thomas Edison. Newton because of the apple falling on his head. Edison because of the lightbulb.

"You should sue the school," Lori told her.

To which Heather replied, "I should thank them. Or at least the maintenance person who did the terrible installation of the bulbs. Because now I see the light."

Pun intended, of course.

Pop psychologists could have a grand old time analyzing what exactly went on with Heather. Coping mechanism to deal with trauma? Actual epiphany? Or good-old fashioned late-stage puberty? It didn't matter. The fact remained. Heather saw some sort of light, and that light guided her down a new path.

Schoolwork still got done, efficiently and effectively, but without any ambitions to write valedictorian speeches or personal statements for Ivies. Piano mastery was supplanted by guitar noodling. Swimming remained important to her, but it became a private endeavor, and rarely in pools. Sometimes people would spot her at the reservoir, far off in the distance, her body racing away from the designated swim area. But she never even entertained the notion of joining the team.

When she became a "party girl" was a matter of interpretation, but by sophomore year, around the time she formed a trio with Buck and Lori, she was a fixture at more social events than extracurricular ones. By junior year, she had acquired a taste for wine coolers and cheap weed. She wasn't against a hazy hookup on a pile of coats, which gave her a certain reputation. And by senior year, she was sneaking into clubs in the city and cementing her status as a paragon of teenage snark and disaffection.

The relationship that had developed between her and Schultz seemed to soften her edges the tiniest bit, or at least enough for her to trust and listen to someone besides her two best friends. Because now, at the pool, when Bev asked who the best swimmer was and everyone turned to Heather, she turned to Schultz.

"I think they want you to see if you can swim to the bottom," he told her.

"To accomplish what, exactly?" she asked.

Trevor was sheepish in his response. "See if there's . . . another way out?"

Saying it out loud did make it sound a bit ridiculous. The situation, however, was beyond ridiculous.

"If that will chill some of you out, fine," Heather said. "I'll try your little free-diving experiment. But I guarantee you that all I'm gonna find is muck and weeds."

Buck raised a hand like he was in class.

"Yes, Charles," Heather said, because Buck's real name was Charles and Heather liked to remind him of that whenever he was being annoying.

"If you're gonna be naked again, then I'm all for it," he said, eyebrows waggling.

Schultz played the part of the supportive boyfriend who scoffed at the notion of jealousy. He put a hand on his heart and said, "I'm all for Heather doing whatever makes her comfortable. Clothed or as God made her."

This made her snort a laugh through her nose. "If I'm descending into the briny deep, I guess I should keep on a layer or two. Could be cold down there."

"Or you might find a magic portal and end up in a land of puritanical pixies or something," Jared added.

"That too," Heather said.

Trevor didn't see it as much of a joke. Forget magic. There actually were natural pools that led to underground caves in the world. Divers who specialized in underwater spelunking explored them. He'd seen an entire claustrophobia-inducing documentary about it.

Heather, of course, had no scuba equipment or goggles. By her own estimate, she could hold her breath for "three minutes, maybe longer," which seemed like enough time to blindly explore the bottom and resurface. But as Heather slipped into the water and prepped for her descent—bobbing on the surface as she rhythmically inhaled and exhaled—Trevor couldn't help but think of another movie.

Fiction this time. But even more claustrophobic. And far

more terrifying. He'd only watched a couple scenes. Didn't even know the title. It was playing on HBO one night during a middle school sleepover at Dan's house. Dan's parents subscribed to all the movie channels, which meant the boys could stay up late and watch "boobie movies," as Dan called them.

HBO didn't show anything nearly as risqué as Cinemax or Showtime, but the boys had clicked over in hopes of catching at least an installment in the Porky's series. What they caught instead was the story of some kids trapped in a cave and a woman (their teacher?) helping them swim underwater from one section of the cave to another. It goes without saying that the swim doesn't go as planned. A kid freaks out and tries to surface too early. The woman gets stuck in the middle and the only way to survive is by sticking nothing but her lips out of the water in a passageway that isn't completely flooded. Why only lips? Because there's only a few inches of air to breathe.

Excruciating. The boys immediately retreated to Cinemax.

Trevor couldn't change the channel now as Heather took one final gulp of a breath, filling her lungs to capacity, and then used the momentum of her bouncing to torpedo herself straight down underwater. The best he could do was turn away. And yet he didn't turn away. He needed to know what was down there.

SHI-WOOOO

The sound marking every two minutes had become part of the background, almost unnoticeable. But Bev noticed it, of course. It reminded her of her hourglass, which needed to be flipped. She did so and carried it over to a stump to set it down.

Trevor turned back to the water. A few bubbles surfaced. Beyond that, there was no sign of Heather. The water seemed blacker than black now, but Trevor figured that his anxiety was playing tricks on his mind. Surely it couldn't have gotten darker.

Silence. Eyes locked on the black hole. Time slowing and speeding up and detaching from their reality. Then a question.

"How deep could it be?" Jared asked. "Even if it's thirty or forty feet, how long would that take?"

No one had an answer. Only the sound.

SHI-WOOOO

At least two minutes now that she was still down. Jared put a hand on Schultz's shoulder, and Schultz reached up and gave him an appreciative pat. Were they feeling what Trevor was feeling? Which was a combination of fear and excitement. He wanted Heather to come back up, but he also didn't. An escape route. That's what he really needed. Not necessarily for right now. For someday soon.

"If she made it out, then I'm not sure I have the breath or the guts to go that way," Bev said, returning from the hourglass.

"If she made it out, she's coming back for us," Schultz said.

Buck bit his lip, didn't say a word. Schultz had gotten to know Heather over the last few weeks, but Buck had been her close friend for years. If his instinct was that she had abandoned them, then she had probably abandoned them.

"She's coming back," Schultz said firmly.

There were no more bubbles in the water. No movement at

all. Trevor pictured Heather gliding through an underground tunnel toward some light. Ending up . . . Well, he couldn't say. Somewhere better? Somewhere far worse?

SHI-WOOOO

More than four minutes now. Probably beyond the limit of how long she could hold her breath. And still no sign of her. This was either very good or very bad.

"Should someone else go after her?" Buck asked.

"If she can't handle it down there, then I doubt any of us can," Sarah said. Her tone was neutral, but her eyes registered worry. Whatever spell the pool had her under was starting to lose its grip.

"If she passed out, she'd float to the top, right?" Bev asked.

"Sounds right," Buck whispered.

"Unless she gets caught under something," Sarah said.

It gave them all some more dread to stew in. Trevor held his breath. Sarah held herself and shivered. Jared paced. Bev joined him. Buck crouched down, touched the water, as if he was checking to make sure it was still there. Schultz balled his hands into fists.

SHI-WOOOO

"Screw this," Schultz said. "I'm going in."

A running start and a dive would be required. He backed up, closed his eyes. "Got this, got this, got this," he whispered through gritted teeth. Then he took off, leaping and fanning his arms out and into a ridiculous, but impressive, swan dive. At the top of his arc, the surface of the water broke. Heather emerged, gasping for breath.

No matter how hard he tried, Schultz couldn't contort his body enough to avoid landing on his girlfriend. As his rib cage crashed into Heather's shoulder, she yelped, and then they both went under.

They both popped up seconds later, and Schultz put his arms around her.

"You little shit," she said, pushing him away, more angry than playful.

"I was rescuing you!"

"You were trying to break my neck!"

Buck waved his hands. "Naw, naw, naw. I'm gonna have to defend the kid. He was genuinely concerned."

"I was fine," she said, pushing her hair away from her face. "But I don't have much to report."

"What do you mean?" Trevor said.

"Swim down, swim left, swim right, nothing," Heather said. "I guarantee you'll lose your bearings in there, because there's nothing to touch, nowhere to go. Darkness all the way down."

Sarah tossed up a hallelujah with her hands. "We're stuck, then. So be it."

"Which way to the bus station?" I ask a man sitting on a bench.

He sips his coffee and looks me up and down suspiciously, almost like he knows me. I do the same with him. Maybe we do know each other. But not anymore.

He points down the street, past the Burger King.

"I've never ridden it, but I think it stops over there."

"Do you know how much it is?"

He shrugs. "Depends on where you're going."

"Not far. To the main station. Downtown."

"I could look it up for you."

"No thanks. I'm fine."

I start to walk in the direction he pointed earlier.

"Are you in some sort of trouble?" he calls out.

I probably am, but I say, "Nope. Just gotta get somewhere. To see someone."

This doesn't stop him from following me.

"Here," he says when he catches up. He hands me a twenty-dollar bill.

"What's this for?" I ask.

He shrugs. "I feel like I know you. And I feel like you need it."

Here

They sat in a circle. Like in kindergarten. Not to smoke pot, though, which was the main reason for circle time of late. It was about democracy.

Trevor was chair of the committee, and he posed the first question.

"Who here wants to know if there's a way out?"

Hands went up in the following order: Trevor, Jared, Bev, Heather, Schultz, Buck, and finally, Sarah.

"Who here wants to spend more time trying to find the way out?" he asked.

Hands: Trevor, Jared, Bev. That was it.

"Who here is scared we won't ever find a way out?"

Hands: One of Trevor's inched up, but that was only to encourage others. He was worried, but not scared. When no one followed his lead, he inched his hand down.

"Looks like democracy has spoken," Sarah said. "We're in no rush, so we can all do what we want."

"Dammit," Bev said. "That doesn't make us libertarians, does it?"

"Anarchists, Bev," Jared said. "We're anarchists now."

"Anarchists don't vote," Buck said. "They anarchize."

"That's not a word," Heather said.

"So how do you propose we anarchize?" Jared said.

"That's the great thing about anarchy," Buck said. "You decide."

With that, Buck stood up and his decision was to walk to a quiet spot next to the trees and lie down for a rest. Heather leaned in and whispered something to Schultz. After giving what she said a fair bit of consideration, he nodded. Then they smiled at each other, and she grabbed his hand and led him to a different quiet spot.

Jared turned to Trevor. "I can help the search in a bit. But I need to swim to clear my head."

"You can say that again," Bev told him, and the two of them headed to the water.

Alone with Sarah, Trevor struggled to make eye contact. He wasn't entirely sure why. Because their priorities were clearly different? Yes. Or because he wanted to kiss her again? Also, yes.

"The time is half past an hourglass," Sarah said. "Whatever that means."

"It means the forever night rolls on, I suppose," Trevor said, and then he finally locked eyes with her.

She smiled. "So, you can pause your orienteering for a little bit, right? To spend some time with me?"

"I think that can be arranged."

Motioning with her head toward the others, she said, "We can nap, we can swim, we can . . . sit alone somewhere private."

It took a millisecond to consider the options, but he paused to seem less desperate. "Option three, please."

His head in her lap, her hand down his shirt, she pulled away from the kiss, but not too far. Sarah's weeping willow hair kept Trevor sheltered and safe. The contours of her face were new to him from this angle. Few, if any, people had ever seen her this way. A privilege.

The hourglass had finished its drip, and no one had flipped it. Not that it mattered. Trevor wasn't even sure he could trust it. The other bottles were always magically refilling themselves with wine. So, what did that mean for Bev's device? It meant it was nearly impossible to say how much time had passed. Sleeping, eating, drinking? All those things felt like leisure now. Ways to be distracted. Not necessities. Who knew how long they'd been kissing. Their hands, exploring. They'd forgotten that the others were even there. At least, Trevor had. It didn't mean they took things the whole way. But there were hints. Unspoken promises. Indications that this was only the beginning.

"It feels right," Sarah said.

"This?" Trevor asked, meaning the moment.

"All of it. Us. Here. All of it."

"Are you okay with me looking?"

"For a way out?"

"I want to be here. With you. As long as I can. But I also need to know."

"If that makes you more relaxed, then fine. I prefer to be Zen about it."

"Have to admit. I'm not even sure what Zen means."

"In the moment?" she said hesitantly. "I don't really know either. I'm not a Buddhist. I guess I'd like to be a Buddhist. Buddhism is cool, right?"

Harder to hold in than a sneeze, Trevor's laugh leaked out the side of his lips, and Sarah could undoubtedly feel the vibrations in his ribs.

Sarah laughed even harder, a friendly volley. "God, I'm such a dork," she said as she flopped onto her back.

"I won't tell anyone," Trevor said.

They nestled into the quiet of the moment, until Sarah said, "I do realize there's gonna be a time when we have to go home. I'm not naïve."

"I never thought you were," Trevor responded.

"People have all sorts of thoughts about me. Some are true. A lot aren't."

"Well, I'd like to get to know all the true things about you."

"I'll tell you one true thing. After this summer, I'm not coming back."

"Coming back here?"

"Anywhere in Sutton. I'll find a job in Rochester or maybe the Finger Lakes. An internship in Manhattan. It will make it easier to move there after I get my degree."

"You want to live in New York?"

"Doesn't everyone?"

Trevor had honestly never considered it. He wanted to live

somewhere nice, and New York City, for all the amazing things there, didn't seem nice at all to him. The graffiti, the drugs, the crime. He'd heard the most awful stories about what happened to people when they walked through Central Park at night. And that was supposed to be the pleasant part of the city!

"Okay. So, you're saying you won't come back at all?" he asked.

She put a hand on his hand, and locked in. "I mean, I don't hate it here. I simply think there are better, or at least different, places out there for me. Maybe I'll stop by Sutton for a weekend every once in a while, but my parents plan to downsize in the next couple years. They'll probably get a place on the Cape, where my mom grew up, so that's where holidays will be."

"Huh. I never knew any of this."

"You never asked."

Fair enough. Trevor didn't know how to respond to that, so he didn't. And Sarah filled the silence.

"What about you?" she asked. "Will you live here forever?"

"I guess I'll . . . I mean . . . I haven't thought about it that much."

"Really? I think about that stuff all the time."

Trevor shrugged. "My parents aren't going anywhere, so I'll be here for the summers and holidays. After college, I'm . . . I don't know. I'll live a good life. I'm pretty sure. I hope. I'd rather not worry about those things right now, but maybe you and I will—"

She didn't let him finish the thought. She squeezed his hand and said, "College changes people. It changed Mike already. It will change you too. And me. So sure, none of us need to have anything totally figured out now, but for me, I've got a general direction I want to point myself in, and it's away from here. That's why this night is important, Trevor. That's why this night needs to last as long as it can."

The information didn't come as a huge shock to Trevor, but it was enough to make him sit up in search of a new perspective. As the blood rushed to his head, he took in their surroundings. The pool was empty and tranquil. Buck had awoken and moved. He was now sitting cross-legged in the grass, sparking up another bowl. Jared and Bev were napping, splayed out near the edge of the water, knuckles skimming the surface.

"Hola!" Buck called out between hits.

And that was when Trevor noticed it.

"Wait. Where are Schultz and Heather?" he called back.

Buck shrugged. "Off doing Schultz and Heather stuff?"

There was nowhere to hide. That was one thing Trevor had discovered about this place. The edges near the forest were shadowy, but the shadows only obscured details. No matter where a person was around the pool, they could be spotted from anywhere else. Unless they had stepped into the forest or ducked underwater.

"Were they swimming?" Trevor asked.

Buck shrugged again. "I was keeping to myself. Eyes closed."

"But did you hear any splashes?"

"Not that I can remember."

All the shouting roused Bev and Jared. They immediately noticed the absences too.

"Where's Heather?" Bev asked.

"And Schultz?" Jared said.

Trevor walked the perimeter of the pool, looking at the water for bubbles and ripples, and scanning the forest for movement. Nothing. Except for Sarah, who was now sitting cross-legged where he'd left her. Eyes closed. Serene. Zen? Maybe not. Does Zen involve talking?

"They left a while ago," she said.

"Wait, what?" Trevor said.

"Where?" Bev asked.

"In the water?" Jared said.

Eyes still closed, Sarah said, "I didn't see or hear. I was a bit occupied. We all were. Napping, and daydreaming, and . . . you know. I only noticed they were gone a little while ago. I thought they might come back. I guess not."

"How long ago was this?" Trevor asked.

"I don't know," Sarah said. "Does anyone have a good sense of time anymore? Has anyone flipped Bev's hourglass lately?"

All the liquid in the hourglass was still at the bottom. Bev held it in her hand, examining it like a dead plant she'd neglected to water.

"I have no idea when I last flipped it," she said.

"So, they could've been gone for hours?" Jared asked.

"Maybe days," Sarah said.

"How's that possible?" Bev said.

"How's any of this possible?" Buck said. "We've gone over it already. Time feels different here. I thought we were all fine with it. I'm fine with it."

"I'm not," Trevor said. "I'm seeing what's down there."

"Me too," Jared said.

Tossing her hourglass to the side, Bev stomped toward them and shouted, "No!"

It was jarring. Bev wasn't a yeller, and this certainly wasn't a yelling place. Even the disagreements so far had been in hushed tones. So this demanded attention.

As she reached them, she said "no" again, not as loud, but just as forcefully. "How do you know you can get back here and show us the way?"

"Because that's exactly what Heather did," Jared said. "She found a way out, but she only shared it with Schultz."

"Why would she do that?" Bev asked.

It was something Trevor hadn't considered until that moment, but it made sense. There was very little privacy at the pool. It wasn't possible to truly be a couple there. And he wasn't simply thinking about sex. He was thinking about all the other special moments, the sharing of things that no one else could see, or hear, or even know about. Before they even kissed, Trevor had that with Sarah. Now he wanted more of it. There were only two ways to get it: leave with Sarah or stay with her and wait for everyone else to leave.

"They went off to whisper sweet nothings and do the dirty," Buck said, a cruder, but simpler, way of putting things.

"They could've told us that," Jared said.

"And I would've asked them to stay," Buck said with a sigh. "Honestly, would've begged them. Without Lori and Heather, I'm like half of who I am. Or a third. Those girls mean the world to me. They know that. That's why Heather didn't give me a chance to stop her. Lori neither."

His voice was cracking, and he sniffled as he stared at his bag of weed, which lay in front of him in the grass where he sat. Before he could pick it up and pack another bowl, Bev stepped over, crouched down, and hugged him from behind. Long and hard. His head sagged a bit but not so much that Trevor couldn't read Buck's lips as he whispered, "Thank you."

"I wouldn't take it personally," Sarah said. "I think they just grabbed their chance when they had it."

"Is that what you and Trevor are going to do?" Bev said, finally letting go of Buck and standing up. "Sneak out on us?"

This broke Sarah out of her Zen pose. She was on her feet instantly and pacing toward Bev. "Hey. That's not fair. This is a place for everyone, and I want to be here with whoever wants to be here. You want to be here, right? With your friends?"

"Of . . . yes . . . I . . . do, but I can't help but think of what's happening out there," Bev said as she stepped away from Buck and closer to the forest. "Like, either the world is going on without us, or we're going on without the world. It's so confusing."

"Only because you're making it confusing," Sarah said as she grabbed Bev's hand. "Come on. Let's swim. It's guaranteed to clear your head. Make you feel better."

Sarah tugged playfully, and Bev pulled back at first, but

the invitation proved irresistible. It was probably the water's influence more than Sarah's, but Bev soon gave in, and in a blink the two girls were wading navel deep. As Trevor watched them, he felt the pull of the water too, and he came to an alternate conclusion.

"Schultz and Heather could've just as easily found that spot in the forest where Lori left," he told Jared. "I mean, it's way more likely they left that way than swimming out of here."

"What are you saying?" Jared asked.

"That we don't need to swim to the bottom if you don't want to," Trevor said.

"Do *you* want to?"

"Not really."

"But should we still . . . join them?" Jared asked, and by "them" he didn't mean Heather and Schultz. Trevor was sure of that. So they made their way to the pool.

They danced. Waltzed perhaps. Or maybe tangoed. Not exactly any of those things, but something similar. Trevor and Sarah, Jared and Bev, hand on hand, hand on hip, spinning and dipping and whooshing through the water. There was no music other than Buck sitting along the edge, skimming his feet, and singing "Box of Rain" and "Wish You Were Here." It was more than enough. Discussions of leaving ceased. Trevor and Sarah didn't even want booze or weed anymore. Only each other. And the moment.

When the dancing ended, they all sat together on the edge, their love of the night and the place rejuvenated. They remembered who they were. No longer seniors, but not yet freshmen. Rare and beautiful creatures who survived on both anticipation and nostalgia.

"Would you do it all over again?" Bev asked. "High school, I mean."

"God no," Jared said.

"Most definitely," Buck said. "College, man, I heard it's better. But it's only a matter of time until I fail out."

"No one fails out of Potsdam," Bev said.

"My lazy ass'll find a way," Buck said.

Out of kindness, Trevor wanted to say this wasn't true, but Buck skipped school more than anyone. He wasn't stupid and put in enough effort to graduate, but without parents nudging him out of bed in the morning, there was little chance he would show up for classes at Potsdam. Even music classes, which was the main reason he was going there, and one of the reasons he was so close to Heather. Those two could sit in her basement for hours with acoustic guitars propped up on their knees, playing tapes, eyes closed, searching for the melodies, rewinding, teaching each other, figuring it out together. He wouldn't have Heather in the fall either. He'd only have beer and pot and parties. So yes, in all likelihood, his lazy ass would find a way to fail out. But Trevor couldn't say that.

"I'd totally do senior year all over again," Trevor told them instead, and he immediately felt a hand on his thigh. Sarah. Instead of the standard pat or squeeze, she gave it a loving rub.

The hand stayed there as Sarah said, "Could you imagine anyone else being here with us? They'd ruin it. This is the perfect group."

"Remember Gina Barnes?" Buck said. "I wonder what happened to that chick. I bet she would've been a fun person to have here."

"I heard she moved to Utica," Bev said.

"I heard she went to juvie," Sarah said.

"Same difference," Jared said.

"Did she really slap Mrs. Carson?" Bev asked.

"Hell yeah, she did, and Carson deserved it," Sarah said. "I was there. I don't remember what Carson said, but she basically called Gina a slut. I would've slapped her too."

"I heard she was a lesbo," Jared said.

"Carson?" Sarah said.

"No, Gina," Jared said. "That's messed up, right?"

"It would mess up any shot I'd have with her, that's for sure," Buck said. "Which was pretty minimal already."

"Not if juvie allows conjugal visits," Sarah said.

No one else was speaking up, but there was something that didn't sit right with Trevor. "Why'd you say it was messed up that Gina might be gay?" he asked Jared.

"I think he actually called her a lesbo," Bev said. "Which I'm not sure is what lesbians like to be called."

"Better than dyke," Jared said with a shrug.

"I don't think you can use that word," Trevor said.

Jared just glared at Trevor.

"I heard that ten percent of people are gay," Sarah said. "There's ninety-something people in our class, so that means, like, eight to ten people in our class. But I can't think of anyone who's officially *out* out."

"Hal Pierson?" Bev said.

"I don't think so," Sarah replied. "I know his parents. They would *not* be cool with it."

"Something like ten percent of Americans are Black, but we only have, like, two Black kids in our class," Trevor said.

"That's because Sutton is super racist," Sarah said. "You wouldn't want to live here if you were African American. And it's not like many people can be secretly African American."

"Someone hasn't seen *Imitation of Life*," Jared said.

"I mean, Jared, you're gay, right?" Buck said plainly.

That shut everyone up. For a long time.

"What?" Jared finally said. "No."

"You never officially came out?" Buck said. "I seriously thought that you did."

"What are you talking about?" Jared said.

Awkward didn't even begin to cover it. A feeling of embarrassment flooded Trevor. But not for Jared. For himself. He had never even considered this as a possibility.

"I mean, it's okay if you're gay," Sarah said.

"I'm not fucking gay!" Jared cried, and stood up. Once he was standing, he didn't seem to know what to do. Storming off didn't exactly work in the present environment. Jumping into the water seemed . . . odd. So he simply stood there.

Bev stood up to join him, put an arm around him. "Oh, babe, you're you. You. Are. You. And we love you, no matter what."

His face soured, and he motioned like he was going to push her away, but he didn't push her away. "I fucked Tracy Hendricks," he said. "So what does that make me? Huh?"

Buck threw his hands up in surrender. "Forget I even brought it up."

Jared's bare toes dug at the earth beneath them. Clearly, there'd be no forgetting it. "I'll fuck Bev right now," he said. "Right here on the ground."

It made Sarah laugh out loud, and made Trevor hide his face.

It made Bev do some actual pushing. "Don't be an ass," she barked as she gave Jared a solid shove.

This time, Jared did storm off. Made a beeline straight for the drinks. With a bottle of Boone's under his arm, he headed to the other side of the pool, where he sat alone, took a gulp, and recoiled from the kick.

"What the hell was that?" Sarah asked.

"I shouldn't have opened my mouth," Buck said. "Story of my life."

"You're fine," Bev said. "You were being honest. He was being an ass. I mean . . . has everyone here wondered that about him?"

Trevor hadn't, but Sarah nodded quickly and said, "Yeah, but I never cared."

"Me too," Bev said. "I thought it was kinda cool, actually."

"I mean, he seems pretty adamant about not . . . you know . . . being that," Trevor said.

"Gay?" Sarah said. "It's not a bad word. My uncle is gay. He has lots of gay friends that I know. Nicest guys I've ever met."

"Present company excluded, right?" Buck said.

"No comment," Sarah said.

"I'm gonna go talk to him," Trevor said.

It was a spontaneous decision. Trevor didn't have any significant personal experience with gay people. At least not beyond small talk and short interactions with a few acquaintances—a middle school art teacher, a clerk at the grocery store, one of his mom's fellow nurses. So, while he wanted to support Jared, he had no idea what to say to him. Something comforting? Distracting? When he reached the other side of the pool and sat down next to him, he didn't have time to say anything at all. Jared spoke, in a soft, contemplative voice.

"Do you think we're dead?" he asked.

"What? No."

"It's like a twist in movies. You know? Turns out people are dead the whole time, and they're ghosts or whatever. I told Buck that, and he seemed to think it was possible."

"We're not dead. Because when did we die?"

"I don't know," Jared said, taking a sip of the booze, and wincing. "First time we went swimming here? Maybe it isn't water in there. Maybe it's like . . . battery acid."

Trevor coughed back a laugh. "That must've been a horrible way for us to go. Our skin looks pretty good, all things considered."

Jared kicked at the water. "I'm only partly joking. 'Cause what are the options? We're either in the regular world, or we slipped out of it, right? If we're in the regular world, our parents would've found us by now. Our cars are still parked out there. It wasn't far to walk here. They would've have found us."

"Good point," Trevor said. "Maybe they have found the cars, but they haven't found *us*. Because they can't find this place. Like, it's only for us."

"But the sun's not coming up," Jared said. "I don't think this place is invisible. Maybe the world is frozen around us. Like in that stupid TV show, where the alien girl stops time with her fingers. Everyone is frozen except her."

"We're the alien girl?"

"Do you have a better explanation?"

"Maybe it's the opposite," Trevor said, because he wasn't above a bit of theorizing. "Like *Jurassic Park*. We're the mosquitoes in the amber. The world is going on around us, but we're stuck in this time. Not growing older at all. If we've been here for days, like Bev says, then why haven't I grown any stubble?"

"Because you're a girly-man?"

"Fine, then Buck. Buck should have a bit of a beard by now. But he doesn't."

Jared considered this for a moment, then turned and looked in Trevor's eyes. "I'm not gay."

Trevor looked back, searching Jared's eyes for a lie, but not knowing whether he wanted to see one. "Okay," he said.

"I don't know what . . . I am," Jared said softly.

"Okay."

"But I don't want anyone to tell me what I am, you know?"

Trevor nodded, but he didn't know. Not really. Trevor was always exactly who people expected him to be. A good student. A reliable athlete. A mostly respectable guy who liked girls, and sometimes those girls liked him back. For years, parents and teachers and friends had been encouraging him to be this way, and so he was. He never saw it as a particularly bad thing. The alternative simply didn't register in his mind all that much.

"The only thing I'm certain of is that I'm being punished," Jared went on.

"Is that what it feels like to you?" Trevor asked.

Jared looked down. "It does right now. But you wouldn't understand."

"What do you mean?"

Jared looked up at Trevor. "You're like this golden boy. The world is never punishing you."

"I'm hardly a golden boy."

Jared tilted his head and cocked his eyebrows in disbelief. "Look at where you live. Where you're going to college. Look at everything about you. You got those 90210 sideburns, and if you're not six feet tall, then you can tell people you are and they'll believe you. You're with Sarah Lawson, for chrissakes. Do you think she'd be with some sad nobody?"

That was a valid point, but Trevor didn't want to fully accept it. Accepting it would mean that any injustice or emotional suffering that he had endured would be considered insignificant, simply because of the hand he had been dealt. That wasn't fair, was it?

"I'm lucky is all," Trevor said. "But we're both lucky. This place is proof. We're the ones who found it. Not anyone else. It's not a punishment. It's a gift."

"Eye of the beholder," Jared said. "That's why I'm thinking about walking into the woods. Seeing what's out there. I don't know, maybe it's worse than here, but I can't hide in that stuff for much longer."

He motioned with his head to the water.

"Do you really believe leaving is the best idea?" Trevor asked.

"Maybe not. But neither is this," Jared said, raising the bottle. "And yet I'm doing it anyway."

With all the strangeness going on, Trevor had forgotten that Jared didn't drink alcohol. Not that Jared needed a reason to abstain, but he certainly had one: his uncle Lance. Jared had only a handful of memories of Lance, because Lance was fourteen years older and died when Jared was four. Driving drunk from a Friday night football game. A VW Beetle. A slippery road. A lamppost next to the movie theater. A stupid decision that still reverberated over a decade later. To this day, Jared would steal car keys from kids at parties if he thought they'd had too much to drink, which gave him the unfair reputation of being a bit of a wet blanket. His friends knew better. Jared didn't judge people who drank. He simply didn't want another family to go through what his family went through. Unsurprisingly, he had never even tasted alcohol himself.

He was tasting it now. Plenty of it. Trevor wasn't sure whether to comment on the fact. So instead, he stayed silent. He reached forward and took the bottle from Jared. It was about a quarter-full and Trevor downed the rest of the sweet concoction in one gulp. It wasn't to impress Jared, but it seemed to impress him. Jared patted Trevor on the back.

After placing the bottle behind them, Trevor reached over and returned the pat.

"I'm not gonna kiss you," Jared said. "So don't get your hopes up."

"Ditto."

Downtown is sadder than I remember, or maybe I didn't see the sadness before. Even on a summer morning, the happiest type of morning, this place is depressing. All boarded-up windows and guys hanging out next to mini-marts.

I'm glad I won't see it for much longer. I switch buses at the main station. Two dollars to get there and then fifteen dollars to head south to a real city, New York City, on something called the Megabus.

A good deal? They tell me it is, but it basically leaves me broke.

Last stop: Port Authority. I've been there before, when I was a kid, and even though I tried not to act scared, I was scared.

Am I scared now? How could I not be?

But I'm also excited. I know when and where I am. And who I need to see.

Waiting Room

The night pressed on. Sarah compared it to being at the ends of the earth. The poles, where winter was pure black for weeks at a time. Obviously not as cold. Or depressing. At least it wasn't for Trevor.

He kept an eye on Jared, who was acting more or less like "himself," wading in aloofness or dripping with sarcasm. Whatever grudges Jared might have held didn't manifest, and he joined in a trio with Buck and Bev, hanging out at one end of the pool while Sarah and Trevor lingered at the other.

"I wonder who's the third wheel," Sarah remarked at one point, and it made Trevor's mind swirl with possibilities. He had never considered that Jared might be gay, so how could he be a good judge of Buck's preferences? And what about Bev? What did she want from a relationship? He didn't have the faintest idea if either guy even registered on her radar.

Every once in a while, Trevor would glance over at Jared and motion his head slightly toward the trees, as if to say, *Heading that way, or what?* Jared would wave him off, or mouth words like *not now* or *I'm okay.* Which comforted Trevor and worried him at the same time. He wanted Jared to stay with them, and yet he also wanted to know that they all had the power to leave whenever they so desired.

That's when the truth hit Trevor. As much as he'd talked about finding a way out, he'd expended very little effort toward that goal. He hadn't stepped into the forest. Or swum to the bottom of the pool. He hadn't conducted any experiments beyond those initial ones. Truth be told, he didn't have the desire to do anything more. He was comfortable. They all seemed to be.

Thoughts of family and other friends flitted in and out of Trevor's mind, never giving him enough time to miss them. A blessing. The night was impossibly long, but in some ways, it still felt like a single night, so Trevor was glad his focus could remain exclusively on enjoying it. The fact that no one had come to find them also didn't bother him. It meant what he wanted it to mean. Since he felt okay, then everything *was* okay. It would all work out in the end. Instead of theorizing about the whats and whys, he trusted this rare and wonderful feeling of contentment. He also trusted that Sarah was staying put. Which meant he was staying put. Leaving Sarah seemed impossible, both emotionally and physically.

So they stayed. And swam. And danced to tunes that Buck hummed or sang. His voice was deep and surprisingly melodious. A pleasure. Buck drank and smoked pot as much as before, but the others didn't bother. The buzz the water gave them was enough. They didn't sleep on regular schedules, but they dozed off occasionally. Losing consciousness for minutes, or hours, or days. It was hard to say. They didn't attempt to track time anymore. The sound that marked two minutes had become white noise. No one cared to know how long they'd been there or when they'd leave.

Until something changed.

A tree fell. Not close to anybody, so no real danger. Terrifying nonetheless. Because it was a massive tree. No sign of rot or even a hint of wind that might've pushed it over. It simply came crashing down.

"Fuckin' A," Buck said. "That didn't happen, did it?"

It was a maple. At least that's what the leaves seemed to indicate. They all knew what a maple leaf looked like—thank you, Canadian flag—but none of them knew much about trees. Except that this one shouldn't have fallen.

"It's an omen," Jared said.

"Of what?" Bev said.

"Of more trees falling?" Buck whimpered and immediately got into the water.

Bev, Sarah, and Trevor quickly followed. It seemed safer there. Backs to one another, they formed a square, watching the borders for any movement. The tree clearly hadn't been cut down. The trunk was broken. Splintered and fresh. But they didn't rule out the possibility that someone—Schultz, Heather, Lori, or another person—was out there in the woods. Nothing sinister necessarily. Perhaps it was an attempt at communication.

As they watched and waited, time drifted. So did Trevor's

mind. To thoughts of memorable hikes in the forest. Of that first night at that first pool, and the stroll down the dirt road with Sarah. It felt like lifetimes ago. Meanwhile, the leaves didn't rustle. Trees didn't sway, let alone fall, which was less than satisfying. With more falling trees, then maybe a pattern would emerge. One falling tree didn't do much more than cloak the area in a new layer of anxiety. Though it was not enough anxiety to keep them in the water.

It was only then that Trevor realized that Jared had never entered the pool. He was reclined sideways on one of the benches, staring at the fallen tree like he was on a couch and glued to the TV. It worried Trevor, so he called out, "You okay?"

This roused Jared. He sat up and slowly ran a hand down the front of his face, like he was milking sleepiness out of it. Then he hopped to his feet and headed toward the fallen tree. His walk was careful, deliberate. He checked his flanks. He held his hands at the ready. When he finally reached his destination, he touched the broken stump.

"Is it warm?" Buck asked.

"Not really," Jared said, pulling his hand away and bringing it up to his cheek.

"Any burn marks?" Bev asked.

"Doesn't look like it," Jared said.

"Does lightning leave burn marks?" Trevor asked.

"Why would it be lightning?" Sarah said. "Did anyone see lightning? Hear thunder?"

No one answered.

Meanwhile, Jared climbed atop the fallen trunk, like

mounting a horse. He petted the bark, leaned forward, and smelled the wood. Then he placed his cheek on it and leaned farther down to press his ear against it, as if checking for a heartbeat. For a long while, he kept it there, and he rubbed his hand on the surface in slow circles. It was strange, almost religious. A ritual of sorts. And if Trevor wasn't mistaken, Jared whispered something to the tree.

"What's he doing?" Bev asked.

No one answered. Trevor's mind didn't wander this time. It was fixed on his friend. If he could even call him that. Could he? Their relationship spanned over a decade, all the way back to elementary school. But Trevor began to wonder how truly close they were. He cared for Jared. Spent so much time with him over the years. Mostly doing nothing but hanging out, joking around. But this place had shown him that Jared wasn't as comfortable sharing certain aspects of his life. At least not with Trevor. He could only blame himself for that.

Watching Jared felt like spying on the neighbors, like sitting next to a darkened window late at night, waiting not for skin, not for murder, but for something to indicate they were boring and relatable people.

Jared was neither of those things as he communed with the tree. Electric and alien. Bewitched in a way Trevor couldn't possibly understand. His eyes were closed, and he was murmuring something. A prayer? A mantra? Though Trevor wasn't a master at reading lips, he was fairly certain that Jared was repeating the same words.

You're right . . . You're right . . . You're right . . .

Had this place done something to Jared? Changed him in some fundamental way? Trevor couldn't say for sure, because he didn't even know the answer when he asked the same question of himself. Trevor didn't feel like a changed person. But does a changed person usually notice the change? Change consumes, regurgitates, and assures you that this is who you are and who you've always been. To spot change, an outside perspective is usually needed.

Trevor knew Jared was smart. And sarcastic, which often goes along with being smart. Cynical yet loyal, at least to some. Bev often spoke of the lengths Jared would go to make sure she was happy. Buying her favorite snacks—Andy Capp's Hot Fries—and leaving them in her backpack. "Helping" her with English papers by slipping handwritten drafts into her locker. Basically, being there for her whenever she needed him. She returned the favor when she could, though perhaps not nearly often enough.

Perhaps not now. Like the others, she simply watched as Jared spoke to the tree. And she didn't move as he climbed off the trunk and stood, arms straight at his side, and stared into the darkness along the edge of the woods.

Once again, "What's he doing?" was all Bev could say.

Jared was the one who answered. "It fell for me," he said. "Get it? The tree *fell*. For *me*. Thank god someone did, right? I knew I was a tree-hugger, but this is ridiculous."

The corny joke made him laugh a laugh so filled with light that it almost brightened the forest in front of him. Trevor wouldn't have called laughing uncharacteristic of Jared, because he'd certainly heard plenty of joy from the kid before. However, this time felt slightly different. It felt like relief.

"Don't worry, I'll be fine," he said, in a comment that seemed directed at Bev. "It was a sign, you know? That this place is all used up for me. The water can't trick me anymore. I know I need to get back and deal with . . . everything. So don't follow. Have your fun while there's fun to be had. I'll see you when I see you."

Then he waved over his shoulder at them and stepped straight into the black.

"Wait," Bev called out. "No . . . I . . . please don't leave me here without—"

It was too late. The forest made a sound when Jared entered, the same soft puff they heard when Lori left. To Trevor that meant one thing. Jared wasn't coming back.

The tunnel reminds me of the way out. I'm not sure if it's the Holland or the Lincoln. Those are the two, right?

There are no flames behind me this time. Nothing—no one—to run from now. Only something—someone—to run to.

I trust the evidence and my instincts, and I don't look back.

Sour Times

The even ratio invited a possibility. A coupling of convenience. Now when Trevor and Sarah shared time together, so too did Buck and Bev. Well . . . not at first. For a little while, they sat or swam alone. But like a couple of kids who aren't necessarily friends at a playground, they drifted toward each other. Quick conversations became leisurely ones, and before long they were sitting face-to-face, cross-legged on a log bench for extended stretches. It progressed to heads on shoulders, hands on hands on knees. It wasn't inherently romantic. Yet the inevitable happened. The rom-com trope of annoyance begetting passion actually delivered.

"Look," Sarah whispered, with her mouth peeking over the edge of the water. "They're smoooooooching."

Her tone was charmingly immature, and it confirmed what Trevor was feeling. Delight and relief. If Buck and Bev were enjoying their time together, it meant they could all make this place work. For as long as they wanted.

That was the hope. Jared's departure convinced them they had a certain amount of agency over how and when they could leave. As the four of them swam together, Sarah related it to mix tapes.

"They're better than actual albums," she told the others.

"Mix tapes?" Buck said. "No. Just no. You're telling me your li'l collection of Tori Amos and Indigo Girls favorites beats *Dark Side*? I'm not buying it."

"Hear me out," Sarah said. "Albums are manipulative. The artists lead you where they want to lead you."

"Yeah," Buck said. "*Dark Side* leads me to bliss."

"He's got a point," Bev said.

"I've got a point too," Sarah said. "Which is control. When you make a mix tape, it's something you do for yourself. It's a reflection of who you are, where you are, and where you want to go. It's all about you. *You* get to choose the order of the songs. You chart the rise and fall of the emotions. When you decide the particular moments when certain songs show up on the mix, then you decide when you're gonna have certain thoughts and feelings. You can even add your own voice between songs, to remind yourself of who you were when you put the mix together."

"Sorta like rap albums?" Trevor asked. "Beastie Boys. N.W.A. They have, like, little skits between songs."

"Yeah, but that's *their* journey, and they're just sharing it with us," Sarah said. "Mix tapes are our own personal journeys."

Buck held up his hand in a sarcastic OK sign, and Sarah slapped it away. Mostly playfully.

"Mix tapes have rules, though," Bev said. "Can't repeat artists. Unless you're going all mellow or all intense, you have to alternate between tempos and moods. Can't have songs with the same name. Unless that's the theme. And if it's got a theme, you gotta stick to it."

Sarah scoffed. "Who says? *You* are entirely in charge of them and can do anything you want with them, which makes them the most meaningful journeys of all."

"But don't you make mix tapes for other people?" Bev said. "You know, to impress them? To manipulate them?"

"She's never made me a mix tape," Trevor said.

"And he's never made me one," Sarah added.

"Well, that's not very romantic," Bev said.

Sarah shook her head. "This. Right now. This is romantic. I know that sounds cheesy, but it's true. Because right now we're all making our own mix tapes. Controlling our own destinies. We can keep the music going as long as we want. Forever maybe."

Buck could've rolled his eyes. Bev could've referred to "rules" again and pointed out that there was only so much room on a cassette tape. An hour. Maybe two, if you record at double speed. Neither bothered, though. Probably because there would be no convincing Sarah that her thesis was silly and there were holes in it, which was the same as convincing her that it was time to leave. Clearly she didn't want that, and neither did the others.

So they swam.

Chatted about meaningful shit and useless shit.

Kissed a lot.

Snacked a little.

Napped.

In their own particular orders.

Buck still drank and smoked, but the others abstained.

They discussed the ones who left, but not by name. Only by concept.

"They're missing so much," Sarah said. "I feel bad for them."

The others nodded in agreement.

Days or weeks or months passed by, and the two couples settled into their corners of the world. When they weren't together on their "double dates," as Sarah called the moments when the four gathered, each couple pretended the other couple wasn't there.

The kissing and touching followed its natural evolution. And on a day without a date, at a time that could never be determined, in the shadows near the spring, Trevor and Sarah finally slept together. It wasn't a moment like the first kiss. There was no melodramatic preamble, no breathy declaration. It simply happened. They were both finally comfortable enough to take things a step further.

It didn't feel strange that it had taken so long to happen. Yes, the act itself had its awkward moments—for instance, trying to figure out the right direction to unroll a condom found in a bottomless box that Schultz had left behind. It was fresh and fumbly, but it also felt like they'd been doing it forever. They were newborn foals miraculously finding their feet. Neither was a virgin, though neither was experienced enough that it made much of a difference. Trevor's relationship with Kelly felt like it was years ago, and he wasn't sure whether the things Kelly liked would be the same things Sarah would like. Those were the only true sober sexual experiences he could draw from.

Of course, like all teenage boys, he had seen some pornography, though not a lot. Mostly *Playboys* and *Penthouses*, and a few grainy, double-dubbed triple-X movies screened surreptitiously in Dan's basement. He had gleaned a few ideas from those, but the rest was primarily improvisation. Trevor and Sarah knew their own bodies enough to hint at what they did and didn't enjoy, or at least at what they thought they did or didn't enjoy. They knew each other well enough to follow simple verbal cues, if not all the subtle signals.

There. No there. Right. Yes. Um. Up. Slower. Yes. Again.

Trevor was surprised he didn't once worry about whether Bev or Buck might be watching. In fact, he assumed they were being distracted by the same thing. Perhaps they were, though he never violated their privacy, and they never talked about sex when they were all together. Soon, what had taken so long to establish itself became a normal part of existence, like everything else that was once new and exciting. Like swimming.

"Are you awake?"

Trevor rubbed his eyes. Rolled over to the left. Sarah was there, but she was sleeping. Or pretending to.

"I'm sorry. I didn't mean to . . ."

Trevor rolled over to the right side. That's where he found Buck, sitting on a bench not far away, leaning forward.

"Hey," Trevor grumbled. "Everything okay?"

"Yeah," Buck said. "I mean . . . yeah. I don't know. Girls are both asleep, so I thought now was a good time to, you know, shoot the shit."

"About?"

"About the girls," Buck said. "Or Bev, specifically."

"I'm not asleep," a voice mumbled, but thankfully it wasn't Bev's.

Sarah sat up.

Buck couldn't face her. Eyes to the water, he said, "Oh, sorry, I . . ."

"I'll leave you two alone if you want," Sarah said, pushing herself to her feet. "But you better not talk trash about my girl."

Buck glanced over to Bev, curled double on the ground at the other end of the pool. His face lit up. Then he finally turned to Sarah. "No, stay. Probably best if I talk to both of you."

Wiping her hands on her shorts and cocking an eyebrow, Sarah said it again. "You better not talk trash."

"Never," Buck said. "I love that chick."

The word was a dagger. *Love.* Neither Trevor nor Sarah had said it yet. Trevor certainly intended to, but only at the right moment. Not before or after sex, when he feared it might come off as cloying. Even though that was when he usually wanted to say it. When he felt closest to her in every way. He suspected that she wanted to say it too. Though he wondered if she'd said it before, to Mike, and carried around regrets about using the word too fast and too freely. Walking on eggshells around such a wonderful word seemed silly, though. Especially when Buck said it so easily.

"Love her, love her, love her," Buck went on. "But, man, I do not deserve her. 'Cause I sure as hell don't get her."

"Is that what you need to tell us?" Sarah asked as she sat back down.

"I don't need to tell you anything," Buck said. "I need to ask you something. From your perspective, has she been acting . . . different?"

"How so?" Trevor asked.

"Like sometimes she only wants to be here with me," Buck said. "Intensely. Other times? Totally distant. Like her mind is trying to . . . fly back home. It's . . . vexing."

As far as Trevor knew, Bev hadn't shared the news about her mom with anyone but him. The girls would often have private chats, out alone, treading water in the middle of the pool. Surely if Bev wanted Sarah to know, she would've told her by now. Probably also would've shared that Trevor was in the loop. But Sarah never mentioned Bev's mom to Trevor, so it was safe to assume that such a conversation never happened. Similarly, if Bev had informed Buck, then he probably wouldn't be having his dilemma. He'd know that she was struggling with her priorities.

Now, it certainly wasn't Trevor's place to share Bev's secret with anyone, and yet he had to tell Buck something.

"Have you thought about the conundrum?" Trevor asked.

"The what?" both Sarah and Buck said.

"If time is frozen here, then it means that any bad things

we have to face in our other life are waiting for us to get back," Trevor said.

"Good things too," Sarah said.

"Sure, but it's only good things here," Trevor said. "On the other hand, if time isn't frozen, then we're missing out on everything out there. Good and bad."

"I've definitely thought about shit like that, but swimming and, you know, just bein' with Bev usually chases those thoughts away," Buck said. "So which option is the right one?"

Trevor knew which one he thought it was, but he wasn't about to determine that for other people, so he shrugged and said, "That's the conundrum. Which option seems better to you?"

Buck chuckled to himself, then declared, "Both are rad. Both also suck balls."

"And maybe that's what she's struggling with," Trevor said, though he didn't need to say "maybe."

"So, what do I say to her?" Buck said. "To keep her afloat?"

It all depended on what Bev truly wanted. Did she want to enjoy herself for as long as possible before facing the tough situation with her mother? Did she want to spend time with her mother before things got worse? Or did she want that whole situation to pass her by? Did she want to return home to a world where that painful moment was long gone? Trevor didn't, and couldn't, know.

Sarah, on the other hand, provided a confident answer. "There are always gonna be bad things and good things waiting," she said. "But like Trevor said, here it's only good things.

Tell her to let the world spin however it's gonna spin without us. We have everything we need here."

Buck dug that answer. It made him smile at least.

Without even thinking, Trevor added one more piece of advice.

"You told us that you love her. Tell *her* that too. Even if you've told her many times already. People need to hear it. And to be reminded."

This made Buck smile again. Because maybe he did love Bev, and even if it was a fleeting feeling, maybe that was all he needed to say to help her.

His smile remained as Buck ambled away. Bev was still sleeping, and he didn't wake her. He swam instead. Elementary backstroke, the stroke of contentment. Something Trevor was thrilled to see. He watched Buck so closely and happily that he didn't notice that Sarah was crying. Not until she leaned into him, forehead to forehead, and he saw the tears streaming down her face.

"Oh man," Trevor said, reaching with a thumb to wipe a tear from her cheek. She grabbed his hand before he could do it, opened it gently, and pressed it against that cheek.

"I love you," she said.

"Oh . . . I . . . I . . . love you too," Trevor replied, instantly regretting his hesitation.

"I'm not saying it to keep you here," Sarah told him.

He believed her. He believed something else too. "But you're saying it because of what I said to Buck, right?"

Sarah pulled away and shook her head. "Yes. And no. I've

wanted to say it. I've been waiting for the perfect moment, and I knew the perfect moment was now. Because you're right. People need to hear it. You need to hear it."

"I love you," Trevor said again. Because people also need to be reminded.

Bev eventually woke, and the two couples settled back into their corners of their odd little Eden. Whispering. Holding each other. Passing time. Everything seemed back to the way it should be. So it came as a shock to the others when, with no warning, Bev simply stood up, kissed Buck on the forehead, said, "Thank you for everything," and paced straight into the forest.

With a puff, another was gone.

Port Authority pulses with potential. Not just for me. For everyone here. The definition of a crossroads.

It's not as scary as when I visited as a kid. Maybe because I'm older and braver. Even if I don't feel like it. I don't know. The obvious homelessness is more distressing than anything. Plus, it makes me think . . .

Am I homeless now? Maybe I am.

Not that it matters. Or at least, it isn't my focus. Neither are all these little computers people are carrying. Though they're definitely off-putting. No, I'm focused on an idea, an absolutely insane idea.

Remember the conversation? About which world was frozen and which one was carrying on? Call me crazy, but I think it might actually be both.

I have to see if she's here.

Mr. Self Destruct

Buck changed immediately. His relaxed demeanor retreated, making room for rage. The fallen tree took the brunt of his anger. He broke branches from it and walloped them against the trunk. When he ran out of branches, he smashed the bottles of Boone's against it, creating gardens of glass that twinkled in the tiki light. Before, the bottles were always full. Now there was no putting them back together, and there would be nothing to drink, unless they wanted to sip from the spring that fed water into the pool.

"What the fuck did she do that for?" Buck screamed. And he kept screaming. Nothing vile, particularly, but his words were full of fury. Frustration. Everything in between.

Trevor and Sarah didn't dare answer. They kept their distance. Because what could they say? Trevor couldn't tell him that Bev probably preferred being home with her mother. He was still bound to her secret. And Sarah was bound to her friend and her friend's clear decision to leave.

When Buck eventually ran out of steam, he slid into the water, an arm and his head draped over the lip of the pool. That's when Trevor decided it was safe enough to approach.

But he didn't get in the water. He sat down in the grass a few yards away, trying to get the kid's attention. Buck's eyes were barely open. Puffed up at the eyelids. Milky and red. Still, the pupils were there, and they were locked on Trevor.

So when Trevor started to talk, saying, "You know, you could—" Buck took over.

"Follow her? Hell no. Obviously not what she wanted. Would've asked me to join her, right? Like fuckin' Schultz and Heather. But she didn't say dick about shit. Just fuckin' walked away. Another Irish goodbye."

"Don't take it personally," Trevor said.

"How else should I take it?" His eyes opened a tad. Glared.

It made Trevor nervous. "This place . . . it's . . ." Trevor paused for a moment. He was going to say that this place made people figure out what was important to them. But he realized how that might make Buck feel. So he reconsidered. "Honestly? I don't know what this place is."

"I know," Buck said. "This place is a fuckin' dream that transforms into a nightmare. Like that." He snapped his fingers. "She doesn't want me, and this place doesn't want me either. Nothing left for me here."

Buck pulled himself out of the pool and didn't even bother drying off. Sending streamers of water behind him, he plowed straight into the forest, moving as fast as Trevor had ever seen him move.

It didn't work. Within moments of entering the trees, Buck was exiting them at another spot. It only fueled his anger. He ran and entered at another point. Same result. Out he popped at a different location, as if ricocheting off a wall. It would've been hilarious if it wasn't so tragic.

"Fuck!" he screamed.

Sarah didn't say anything. She simply chewed a thumbnail and watched.

"Sit down," Trevor told him. "Take a moment. Breathe."

"No!" Buck said. And he tried again, plowing into the forest.

This time, a tree came down. An absolute thunderous crash. Close enough that Trevor and Sarah had to scurry back and dodge the flying debris. Buck emerged not far from where it fell, and he stopped for a moment and eyed it with disdain.

It didn't dissuade him, though. After giving the fallen tree a dismissive little kick, he rushed back into the forest.

Crack!

And *Boom!*

Another tree down, then Buck reemerged, even more frustrated.

So he tried again. *Boom!*

And again. *Boom!*

And again. *Boom!*

And . . .

In all, ten trees fell to the ground, which sent Trevor and Sarah diving into the water, like sailors escaping the falling masts of a cannonballed ship. When Buck was sweating and doubled over and panting, he finally gave up, and plopped down despondently in the middle of the wreckage. That was when the demolition appeared to end. And Trevor and Sarah surfaced, shaken.

"Are you okay?" Sarah asked.

Trevor wasn't sure who she was asking. But Buck was the one who answered. "No," he said as he lay on his back. "I've never been okay. I'm this big fuckin' slob. Everyone knows that. That's why they like me. Because I make them feel better about themselves. All I've had is one stroke of luck in my whole entire life. Now it's gone. Ain't ever gonna happen for me again."

"Sure it will," Sarah said.

"Here?" Buck said. "How is it ever gonna happen here?"

There was no good answer to that. There was no indication that anyone else would ever show up at the pool. And a pairing of Sarah and Buck was not even worth entertaining as far as Trevor was concerned.

"Obviously, no one wants me back there," Buck went on, jabbing a finger toward the forest. "That's a place for Bev. And Jared. Schultz and Heather. Lori. People who got a future. You two. You two should be back there. Your whole fuckin' lives are ahead of you. Beautiful babies and Pulitzer Prizes. Me? I've lived the best part of my life here. Back there I'm just a burnout."

Trevor didn't want this to be true. Yet sadly, he knew it was possible. There were guys who went to his high school ten, or twenty, or even thirty years before him, and he'd see them at Mahoney's or Charlie T's, and they'd be sitting at the bar, ruddy-faced and sad or angry or sleepy, depending on the hour of the day. Sure, their faces would light up when someone they recognized would step up to buy a round of drinks, but none of those people stayed long enough to really talk. There'd be exchanges of "how are things?" and "it's been ages" and then the people with bigger and busier lives would escape back to the tables with their families or coworkers.

"I'm sorry," Sarah said to Buck.

"You didn't give me this life," Buck replied. "You didn't make her leave."

"I gave you bad advice," Sarah said. "The moment any of us starts even thinking about what's out there, it's over. Our mind can't wander from here."

"So what do we do?" Buck asked.

"We block all that garbage out, and we keep going?" Sarah said, clearly unsure of the words herself.

Buck sighed and grumbled as he pulled himself to his feet, then trudged away.

The night trudged too. Trevor and Sarah spent their time distracting each other, trying to ignore the heavy fog of disaffection, while Buck wandered the graveyard of trees. He didn't sing or hum like he used to. Didn't talk to himself. Didn't even smoke. If there had been tears, Trevor might've called it grieving, but there were no tears. Buck simply paced back and forth, occasionally stopping to sit or lie down. Sometimes to doze off.

"Could we carry him out of here?" Trevor asked once when he spied him sleeping. "I don't think he can stay."

"That seems too risky for all of us," Sarah said. "Plus, I doubt it would work. To be able to leave, you have to really want to leave."

"I mean, that's what I figured, but how do we know that for sure?"

"Because he told me."

"Buck?"

"No, the guy. On the trail. When we first got here. The one you asked about before."

It felt so long ago that Trevor could barely picture the dude. Skinny? Seemed right. Jean shorts? Maybe. Towel draped over his shoulders? Definitely. Those were the only physical traits he remembered. But the moment? That was clear in his mind. The bend forward. The whisper. The sharing of a secret.

"Wait," Trevor said. "You said he just told you to have fun."

A guilty smirk. A turn away. "Well, I guess he said a little more than that," Sarah replied. "He said, 'You can only leave when you want to, so enjoy it while you've got it.'"

The last part sounded to Trevor like what Jared had said when he left. It also sounded like the things all his older relatives told him as he neared graduation. Even cousins in their twenties pretended like they were wizened sages in that regard. Eat, drink, and be merry, because tomorrow you have to . . . work a crappy job.

This was preaching to the choir when it came to Sarah, obviously. Though Trevor could never imagine her accepting a bad lot in life. Even in high school she had the coolest jobs. Video store clerk at Wegmans and lifeguard at Green Lakes were the most notable, but even those bored her. She always quit within a couple months.

"Did the guy tell you who he was?" Trevor asked her.

"Nope."

"Or how long he'd been here?"

"I think he came from biblical times."

As annoyed as he was at Sarah for keeping this additional information from him, Trevor couldn't help but smile at this. "Did Moses wear jean shorts?"

"No, but I'm pretty sure his brother, Aaron, did."

"Weirdo does have two *a*'s at the beginning of his name. No surprise he'd wear jean shorts."

They giggled for a moment, until Sarah's giggling got a little teary. "I'm sorry I didn't tell you that before. I didn't want you to leave. But it's bound to happen, right? And when you do leave, I'll do my best . . . my best not to be like him."

She motioned with her chin to Buck, still sleeping near the edge of the pool.

"Who said I'm leaving?" Trevor asked.

"You used to say it all the time."

"Well, I'm not saying it now."

Buck didn't appear to get any better. If anything, he seemed to get worse.

On a rare occasion when Buck was awake, Trevor called

out to him from the water. "You should swim. It always makes me feel better."

Buck didn't say a word in response, though he clearly heard Trevor. This became his default. Whenever Trevor and Sarah would try to talk to him, he'd walk away, and whenever they approached him to ask for help cleaning up the fallen trees that were impeding their walks to and from the pool, he'd ignore them. So, they did the job themselves, breaking off whatever branches they could and then burning them in what soon became an eternal campfire.

They had built the campfire halfway between the pool and the trees, lighting it with a tiki torch and marveling at its dancing flames and lack of smoke. It was a welcome addition to the scene, and when they weren't swimming, Trevor and Sarah spent most of their time next to it. Buck didn't join them, of course. He stayed as far away as possible, sitting on the ground at the other side of the pool and staring into the dark forest or up into the blank sky. After a while, they stopped even attempting communication with him. Why bother explaining that the power to leave was in his hands? Nihilism had gotten the best of Buck. He didn't seem to care at all.

Or maybe he cared far more than they realized. Because when he finally rejoined them, appearing at the other side of the fire, there was a clear shift in his demeanor.

Trevor was poking at the embers, and so Sarah noticed Buck first. She offered him a seat on the log next to them, which he accepted. Then he fixed his eyes on both of them, as if preparing for an interrogation.

"Are either of you religious?" he asked.

Trevor had been to a Lutheran church a few times with his grandparents, but he didn't think that counted, so he said, "No."

"I went to Sunday school," Sarah said. "But nothing beyond that."

"My family's Catholic, so you know what that means," Buck said.

"That you need to confess something?" Sarah asked. "Say a Hail Mary or two?"

Buck sighed. "It means I know where we are. Purgatory."

"You think we're being punished?" Trevor asked. "That's what Jared thought."

"Cleansed before meeting God," Buck said. "It's different."

"So we're dead?" Sarah said.

Buck was matter-of-fact. "Yeah. Doornails. There's a reason I haven't be able to leave. I got no future out there. Or here. Isn't that obvious?"

"I don't think it's obvious," Trevor said.

"Then you're not thinking straight," Buck said.

"If that's really the case, then what do you propose we do?" Sarah asked, and she didn't seem to be humoring him. There was concern in her voice.

"Come to terms," Buck said simply. "Make your peace. Or you'll be here forever."

There was no swearing, no joking, nothing at all about how Buck was speaking that indicated this was the same guy Trevor was accustomed to. Perhaps he was spiritual and contemplative like this in private, with his family and closest friends. It didn't matter really. This was who he was at this moment. And at this moment, Buck decided to leave.

First, he gave them both hugs and told them, "Good luck getting right." Then, instead of running, he strolled toward the forest. At the edge, he stopped and turned. For a few moments he surveyed the place he was leaving. Satisfied, he kissed his fingertips and held them up. As Buck entered the forest, Trevor heard the sound that meant only one thing.

He and Sarah were finally alone again.

A metaphor is staring me right in the face. A map of Manhattan shows the Harlem River breaking off from the Hudson at the northern tip of the island. It flows south into the East River, which joins back up with the Hudson at the southern tip. At Water Street.

This map? It's me. Isn't it?

Two lives that were once one life. A coursing river split by a rock. But does the water meet again?

I guess we're gonna see.

Only Shallow

This wasn't purgatory. This wasn't death. Trevor was sure of it. And he wasn't going to entertain any other religious explanations. He was going to appreciate this place for what it now was.

Theirs.

That night when Trevor had joined the others for bowling—however long ago that was—marked a turning point. Outsiders had invaded the tiny swath in the universe he had established with Sarah. Which was entirely his fault. Because he was upset. And, yes, jealous. Because he wanted so much more. Now he had so much more, and he wasn't going to let anyone, or anything, jeopardize that.

They added no wood to it, and yet the campfire burned on. There was nothing to drink or eat, but that didn't matter. There was the pool and their bodies, and that was enough.

Days. Weeks. Years. Impossible to know.

Everything melted into everything else, and Trevor's memory started to slip.

Swim. Sex.

Swim. Sleep.

That was pretty much it.

At least for him.

Sarah would go off on her own sometimes. For walks along the edge of the forest. Sometimes for jogs. Trevor didn't keep track. When she wasn't by his side, he swam or stared at the fire. He enjoyed those times alone, because when Sarah reappeared, it was as if she were coming home from school, or work, or vacation. Expected, yet it still felt like a wonderful surprise.

When she was with him, the talks they used to thrive on—the quips, the confessionals—started to fizzle away, replaced not by mundane discussions but by silence. For long stretches of time. Trevor read this as a sign that they were finally perfectly comfortable with each other and this unique existence. Yet still, occasionally, he had an itch, a desire to simply ask Sarah, "What are you thinking about?"

After resisting the temptation for so long, he gave in, for no reason other than he wasn't strong enough to resist it. They were lying on their backs, between the trunks of two fallen trees, when he said it out loud. Sarah responded immediately.

"We never finished."

"There's nothing to finish here," he told her.

"No, I mean back there. In the other world. There were still a few other pools to swim."

The past was only occasionally on Trevor's mind. Not in a regretful way, though. It was more akin to nostalgia than anything. He had certainly thought about their quest to conquer all the pools, but he had never focused on its lack of completion.

"Does it matter now?" Trevor said.

"I don't know," Sarah replied. "I guess not. But doesn't it bother you a little?"

It didn't bother him at all, but he told the whitest of lies to set her at ease. "It kills me that we didn't finish. But I prefer this. Don't you?"

"Sure."

The silence reestablished itself, and Trevor didn't think much more about it.

But later, the temptation returned. So did the question.

"What are you thinking about?"

"About my favorite movie."

"What movie is that?"

"You don't know?"

While he considered guessing—*The Graduate? Silence of the Lambs* maybe? (It couldn't be *Dirty Dancing* or *Grease*, could it?)—he decided it best to claim ignorance. "Tell me."

She sighed and then she said matter-of-factly, "Heineken? Fuck that shit. Pabst. Blue. Ribbon."

Still no clue.

The floodgates were open. The temptation would not be denied.

"What are you thinking about?"

"Cheese."

"What about it?"

"That I love it."

"Oh."

"I love it so much."

"What are you thinking about?"

"Wind."

"Like air?"

"Yeah. I'm thinking about how it works."

"Fronts, right? Cold and hot."

"I guess. There's no wind here, you know? Not even the gentlest of breezes."

"Yeah."

"What are you thinking about?"

"Your hair."

"Okay. Do you like it?"

"Of course. But you'll lose it someday. Like your dad."

"I won't lose it here."

"I guess so."

"Besides, I think baldness comes from the mother's side."

"Does she have brothers? Are they bald?"

"I won't lose it here."

"What are you thinking about?"

"Game-winning basketball shots."

"Okay."

"What do you imagine it's like to sink one?"

"Probably exhilarating."

"Some people sink only one in their entire lives. Some people, like Michael Jordan, sink a bunch. But it's still exhilarating even after a bunch, I should hope."

"Almost everyone doesn't sink any."

"True."

"What are you thinking about?"

"The story."

"Which story?"

"Our inspiration. 'The Swimmer.'"

"Oh, right, Carver."

"Cheever."

"Right."

"You didn't read it, did you?"

"Not yet."

"So you don't know how it ends?"

"Don't spoil it. I'll read it."

"Um . . . when?"

"Oh. Yeah."

"He swims home. But home is . . ."

"Home is what?"

"You know that I was never swimming home, right?"

"What are you thinking about?"

"The conundrum."

"The what?"

"You're the one who brought it up. With Buck, remember?"

"Oh, right."

"What do you believe? Is the world out there frozen? Or going on without us?"

"I mean, frozen. Clearly."

"Why?"

"Because the other option, where I'm missing out on college and family and everything, well, that's terrifying. Terrifying isn't supposed to happen to guys like me."

"Guys like you?"

"Guys, that, you know, do everything right. Things are supposed to be okay for us."

"Sneaking into pools isn't doing everything right."

"True. Momentary lapse of reason."

"That lasted all summer?"

"It was a long moment."

"Being with me isn't doing everything right."

"Sure it is."

"And what about girls like me? Can terrifying happen to girls like me? Will I be okay?"

"I . . . don't know."

"I'm thinking there's a third option. Besides being frozen or continuing on."

"Don't say purgatory."

"What if it's both?"

"I don't see how that's possible."

* * *

"What are you thinking about?"

"It doesn't matter."

"Are you sure?"

"I'm sure."

"I really want to know."

"I don't think you do."

"Try me."

Sarah reached forward and petted his hair. Looking into his eyes, she asked, "Do we know each other?"

"I mean . . . yeah, of course. I know you better than anyone."

"Do you?"

"Yeah."

"Then why do you ask what I'm thinking about so much?"

"Well . . . I'm not a mind reader."

"Of course not. It's . . ." She stood up.

"Everything okay?"

"I'm going for a walk."

The warning signs were there. Trevor simply refused to see them. The obvious ones were in Sarah's behavior. She slept more and spent more time alone. She almost never swam anymore. When Trevor touched her, she didn't flinch or pull away. But she was slower to return the touch. Jokes didn't come as easily to her. Trevor wouldn't have said she was sad. Then again, he didn't expect her to be sad. This was what they both wanted, right?

Subtle clues appeared in the trees. Discolored leaves. Bulbous growths on the bark. Small dead branches, gray and easy to snap. But Trevor spent so little time along the edges of the forest that he didn't really notice such things.

Sarah must have noticed. When she went out for walks or jogs, she was as close to the forest as possible, skirting the edge, running her fingers along the trunks like they were fence pickets. She told Trevor that she was doing it for exercise, but he didn't understand the need. He rarely exercised because he didn't get fatter or feel particularly antsy. Swimming, and sex, were usually enough for him.

After one of her many loops along the edge of the forest, Sarah sat down next to Trevor, who was poking at the fire and marveling at the dance of flames.

"No river is ever the same river twice," Trevor said, as Sarah settled in. "Same is true of fire. Always different."

"I had a friend in middle school," Sarah said. "Jennifer La-Sorda."

"I remember."

"In the summer before high school, she told me that she didn't like me anymore. She said I was fidgety and restless and it made her anxious."

"Really? I didn't—"

"She was probably right. I called her constantly, to the point that she stopped answering the phone. Her mom or dad would answer it, and I would hang up without saying anything because I was sure they wouldn't pass the message along. They probably knew it was me who was hanging up, which only made things worse. After that, I'd ride by her house on my bike, multiple times a day. At first, I was hoping she'd randomly poke her head out. When I knew she wasn't going to, I did it anyway, because I felt the need to do something. Anything. To fill up my day, my noisy head. Eventually, she just told me that we couldn't be friends anymore. She called me sad. She said that I made her sad."

"How could you make anyone sad?"

"When you leave, don't tell me why or when or how," Sarah said with a sigh. "Just slip out, okay?"

"What?" Trevor sat up straight. "I've already explained this. Those thoughts are so far from my mind."

"Really?" Sarah said. "I figured you'd be sick of me by now."

He leaned over and kissed her cheek. "Never."

"You will be," she said. "Someday. Probably soon."

She sounded so sure of it.

"I would try to work through things," he said. "With you."

"That would make it worse," Sarah said. "Leaving is best."

"But when we leave, if we leave, we're going together, right?"

Sarah shrugged.

This bothered him. There was no way it couldn't. But it bothered him for the wrong reason. He thought that she didn't trust him. Or believe in his love.

So, he told her that he loved her every chance he got. He held her tighter. When there was silence, he didn't fill it with questions. He sang to her. Songs they both loved, but mostly "their song."

Nightswimming, deserves a quiet night . . .

She'd smile, but she wouldn't sing along. Wouldn't even hum. Instead of asking what she was thinking, he asked her how she was feeling, what he could do for her, what would make her happy. She responded with platitudes like, "You've done so much already. Right now, I feel like the luckiest girl in the world."

Unfortunately, Trevor didn't see them as platitudes. He saw them as hope.

There are no phone books. No pay phones either. At least not any I could find. So, I go to the library. The big one with the lions in front.

I tell a librarian who I'm looking for, and she eyes me with suspicion.

"Is this someone who wants to be found?" she asks.

I shrug.

"You haven't googled her?" she asks.

"I don't know what that means," I tell her.

Now she eyes me with more suspicion. And then, after looking at the clothes I've been wearing for god knows how long, she eyes me with an ounce of pity.

"There are some computers back here," she says.

Good Morning, Captain

All the hope in the world couldn't keep the forest from burning. Claws of flames reached toward the pool while the smoke pulsed upward. Trevor had no memory of the fire starting, so he assumed it happened when he was sleeping. His first instinct was to run, and that embarrassed him. Not because the fire surrounded him on all sides and made escape impossible. But because it exposed him as a coward. His second instinct was to look for Sarah.

Where was she?

There weren't many places she could go. The forest was a chaos of flame. In the past, Trevor could never see beyond its wall of black. Now a wall of orange and red obscured his view. Unless she had left before the fire—which he wasn't ready to accept—there were only two other options.

She had burned up—a ghastly, unacceptable thought—or she had made it to the pool.

He dove into the water. The golden hue made it easier to see beneath the surface, but he didn't need to see. He had traversed this pool so many times that he could do laps with his eyes closed and glide over every square inch. Sure, Sarah was an even better swimmer than he was, could hold her breath for minutes at a stretch, but as long as he kept swimming, he would find her in the water eventually.

So Trevor piled on lap after lap, sidestroke so his head stayed above water and he could holler her name with each pulse. "Sarah!

Sarah!

Sarah!"

He yo-yoed across the pool at a speed that he couldn't possibly maintain. That he didn't maintain. Even though the smoke was mostly climbing upward into the starless, moonless sky, there was enough swirling around the surface of the water to irritate Trevor's lungs. After three full circuits of the pool, he had to stop and cling to an edge.

As he coughed, his head swiveled frantically from side to side. He couldn't yell her name anymore, but even if he could, what use would that be? It was time to accept the truth.

A world of ash and water. That was all that was left for Trevor. As wood smoldered, he surveyed the damage. Damp, trudging, not quite defeated. But almost. He felt truly tired for the first time since he'd arrived. Both emotionally and physically. Yet he didn't rest. He couldn't rest. Not that he was going to pitch a fit, like Buck. Instead, he was going to launch an investigation into the source of the blaze. The tiki torches? The campfire? Sarah?

The third option seemed impossible. But so did the other two. The torches and campfire were far removed from the forest, and there wasn't any underbrush to ignite in between. In fact, forest fires of any size were unheard of around here. Too green. Too wet. Too Northeastern.

It must have been started from the outside, by some unseen force. Spontaneous combustion. Like the trees falling, it was simply time for the forest to catch fire. This wasn't exactly a satisfying answer, but it was the only answer that made sense to him.

Which led him to seek another, more important, answer: Did Sarah leave before the fire or because of the fire?

Either option was devastating. Both meant she didn't want to be with him anymore. But the second option was worse. She wouldn't leave him in mortal danger, would she? Maybe she would. Trevor's first instinct was to escape when he saw the fire, wasn't it? Maybe hers was as well. Shameful, but understandable.

It all should've added up to the same conclusion: It was time to leave. And yet, Trevor still had no desire to leave. Simple as that. Whatever Sarah wanted in a fleeting moment wasn't important to him. All that mattered was what *he* wanted.

To be with her. To be. With her. But not out there. Here, and only here. Their special place. Where they'd made a life. The trick was to bring her back, to convert everything to its former state so she had no choice but to return.

He swam and he thought. How on earth was he supposed to do that?

Embers in the forest provided a dull glow, revealing that all the trees were black and charred. So too were the fallen trunks and the benches. Everything else was gone, ash. Except for the glass from the bottles Buck had broken. A lot of it had melted together into strange bubbled and twisted shapes, almost like conch shells. Trevor collected chunks that fit comfortably in his hand. Figuring they might make good tools, he chipped away at them with rocks, sharpening their edges. Soon he had fashioned carving and digging instruments that existed somewhere between the modern and caveman eras.

Even though he didn't have a plan, he began cutting into some of the burnt logs, hacking away at their charred bits as if they were stubborn rinds on delicious fruits. As he did this, his mind tried to rearrange itself, sifting through the clues he had misread and giving them new, truer meanings.

This couldn't have been an impulsive decision. Sarah must have been planning to leave, though she had never said it explicitly. Maybe her constant worrying about Trevor abandoning her should've sparked suspicion. Maybe her mood that seemed to quiet over time should have rung alarm bells. Maybe the fact that she had told Trevor that she loved him, but only told him once, should've clued him in to the fact that things were going south. Certainly, her pacing and jogging and constantly moving about was evidence of her dissatisfaction. And wasn't this place, this lonely place, a dead giveaway? How could anyone really want to stay here?

Trevor didn't have a great answer to that, and yet he still didn't want to leave. And he no longer wanted to stew on the details of why she left. He merely wanted her back. So he attacked the charred remains of logs until he reached their milky brown cores. When thoughts of the past invaded his mind, he became more focused on his tasks, and eventually those thoughts were replaced by thoughts of wood. Nothing but wood. He sawed through it with the jagged glass. He chopped at it. Gouged. Shaped the branches, logs, and stumps. When he managed to detach pieces from fallen trees, he dragged them over to the pool, where he washed them. Some pieces were too big to drag, so he dug the center out of a small log. Turned it into a bucket. Soon he could scoop water from the pool, carry it over to the large pieces, and wash away charred bits.

Meanwhile, something curious happened. Trevor didn't notice it at first, because his mind was set on its singular purpose. But as he whittled the fallen and scorched trees down to their cores, saplings started to sprout along the edges. And the scorched trees that had managed to stay standing finally quietly crumbled into ash, like the long tails of cigarettes given a tap by a finger.

When Trevor did eventually realize what was happening, the forest was well on its way to reestablishing itself. Meanwhile, his work was yielding incredible results. The benches that the fire had consumed were replaced by rough facsimiles he had created.

It should've worried him. To be so obsessed with a task that he didn't realize there were actual trees growing around him? That was beyond odd. He accepted it, though, just as he accepted every strange occurrence he had confronted here. All he cared about was returning this place to how it was when he first came upon it.

He didn't age. Didn't grow a beard. Didn't eat. Hardly slept. He continued to swim, or at the very least, he kept scooping the water, splashing it on his body and the wood. He kept honing the wood, until the benches looked exactly as he remembered them. Then he moved on to constructing the tiki torches. It was trial and error—shaving and turning and rubbing handmade dowels until smooth—and he wasted far more than he used. But he kept at it, and even though he had no oil to fuel them, as soon as he finished the torches and drove them into the ground, flames bloomed at their tips.

By now, the saplings were full-grown trees. All the ash and charcoal had either been washed away or joined with the dirt. The pool had indeed regained its original splendor. And Trevor had nothing left to do but wait.

He swam laps, rarely even touching the edge of the pool. He didn't need to watch the forest. He didn't even need to keep his eyes open. If Sarah were to return, she would head straight for the water, and he would hear the splash. He was sure of it.

Back and forth, back and forth. A rhythm so consistent, it cleared his mind, and on that blank slate, a realization was written.

She wasn't coming back.

Not now. Not ever.

Because why would she?

No one else had.

And how could she?

If time out there was frozen, like he had told Sarah it was, then it would mean she, and everyone else, was waiting for him on the other side, ready to rejoin the world together. They'd have no chance to return because they'd be glued to that moment. Which didn't sit right with him now. That was clearly not what she, or the others, wanted when they left. They wanted to follow their own paths. Leaving this place was never about keeping the group together.

Which left Trevor with the second option. Out there, the world was moving on, and that world was obviously a better place for Sarah—for all of them—and they were more than happy to live in it without Trevor. The same could be said for his family and his other friends. In short: He had been forgotten. Because why would people remember him? Had Trevor really made his mark? For so long he had been worried that he might forget people like Lori, but perhaps his name and accomplishments would be swept like crumbs of memories out of his classmates' minds. It was possible that people like Lori or Buck—or maybe even Jared—might never think of Trevor again.

Such notions were humbling. But also didn't sit right. Sure, he might be forgotten by some. His family, though? Sarah? Impossible. There was a reason no one was looking for him, and it wasn't because no one cared.

So, what about option number three? Sarah had said, "What if it's both?" In other words, the world was frozen, *and* it was continuing without him. He didn't understand that idea when she said it, and he didn't understand it now. He didn't, he hated to admit, understand her. *Her. Sarah.* The person. The soul. The one who left and never gave him a reason why. Maybe he never would understand her. At least not in the ways he wanted to. In the ways that others understood her.

Yet, there was one thing he did understand. He couldn't stay here trying to recapture what they had, waiting on someone who would never return. His life couldn't be defined by this one person, this one place, this one moment. Because the moment was over, and it was okay for things to be over. It was also okay to feel scared and ashamed and unsure about what might come next, as long as he could face what came next. And what came after that.

There was an obvious truth that Trevor hadn't been willing to accept until then. Yes, Sarah had left him. But he was the one who made the decision not to join her. If he had been ready to be with her—out there on the other side with its own uncertain and volatile brand of magic—then the forest would have opened up for him too instead of bursting into flames. It would have guided him away from here. Like it did with everyone else.

Trevor had always taken pride in being a cautious person, which was a much easier thing to call himself than a coward. Even though *coward* often felt like a more accurate word. While he wanted to say that Sarah had cured him of his cowardliness, he couldn't. Because *she* couldn't. Besides, he didn't know if he was cured. All he knew was that he was ready. To leave this life and step into whatever life was waiting for him. If he wanted to be any sort of person worth knowing, let alone remembering, he couldn't simply sit back, be cautious, and hope that things would work out.

He stopped swimming, held the edge of the pool, gazed out to the forest, and saw something he hadn't seen in ages. A trail, clear as clear. Reaching out through the trees, a pathway home.

The water couldn't hold him anymore, couldn't enchant and distract him, couldn't convince him that there was this and only this. Without hesitation, he pulled himself out of its grip and onto the grass. He walked to the edge of the fresh-faced forest. Didn't bother looking back. One foot forward was all it took.

One hopped turnstile and a twenty-minute subway ride later, I'm in Brooklyn. This is my first time here, and I'm sitting at an outdoor café, drinking a coffee that cost me my last three dollars. Evening is on its way, and caffeine is probably the last thing I need, but I also don't have any desire to sleep. Plus, it tastes amazing.

I'm not sure this is exactly how I imagined Brooklyn would look. I expected . . . grittier? This neighborhood is nice. All brownstones and restaurants. Bustling. I suppose that's good.

This is where she lives. At least according to the computers in the library. Those were impressive. The entire world at my fingertips, as they say. Which meant I could look up information on the others as well.

Bev is in Portland, just as Pyper told me. Oregon, though. Not Maine, like I assumed. Works for a big company, doing big company things. But that was all I could find about her.

Heather and Schultz didn't stay together. Or at least they got married to different people and live in different cities. Philadelphia and Baltimore. Which are kinda close, right? I don't know, maybe they meet up and have affairs. People do things like that.

Jared isn't holed up in a cabin somewhere. He's in New York too, but Queens, which the subway maps tell me is northish of here. He founded a nonprofit organization that focuses on alternative forms of transportation. Bikes and whatnot. Seems like a good fit for him.

Couldn't find anything on the computer about Buck or Lori, but I didn't exactly know what I was doing, and it's not like I saw any obituaries or anything. They're probably fine. Out there, living their lives. Rambling on.

It doesn't really matter. I'm not here for them. I'm here for her and only her.

I've got a good view of her apartment. It's on the third floor, and I can't imagine it's very big because the building isn't very big. I guess I always knew that writing jobs don't pay for mansions. It's a relief, in a way. Selling out sucks.

All I need to do is see her, to know if she's happy. Then I can move on. Will I be able to tell that by looking at her? Or will I only see an idea of a person rather than an actual person?

No. I'll see her. Because I know her. I finally know her.

So I wait.

Graceland Too

"Hey, is this the way to the pool?" a girl asked.

Walking toward Trevor on the trail, she was dressed in a purple V-neck T-shirt and a pair of white jean shorts that were rolled halfway up her thighs, hiding the frayed edges.

Trevor nodded and was about to sneak by her without a word, but she had more questions.

"Is it, like, super big?"

"It's . . . yeah, a good size," he said, hearing his own voice for the first time in forever. It sounded, for lack of a better word, young.

"Is it crowded? Or will we have it to ourselves?"

He stopped about five yards away from her. "How . . . how . . . many of you are there?"

She shrugged and pulled something out of her pocket. It looked like a red deck of cards, but it was shiny on the front. When she tapped a finger on it, it lit up. Trevor was too far away to see anything more than the light. It was entrancing all the same.

"Crap, no service," the girl said. "But I'm thinking there'll be at least eight of us, unless I missed a message or two."

"There's plenty of room for eight," he said after clearing his throat. "You should have it all to yourself."

"Great," she said. "If you see anyone else on the trail, don't tell them you saw me, okay? I wanna surprise 'em."

"No problem," Trevor said as he started moving again, walking around her, giving her a wide berth. He walked as quickly as possible because the whole encounter was making him uncomfortable, but he knew he still had to let her know one thing.

She was almost out of view, so he called out to her. "You get to decide what it means to you. Also when to leave. Make the most of that."

If she heard him, she didn't acknowledge it. And now he was hoping that she didn't hear him. The advice sounded so trite. Even if it was the truth.

Not even the hint of a parking lot remained. Only a pickup truck perched halfway in a ditch along the side of the road. The Rat was nowhere to be seen, which was unsurprising. Even though he couldn't put his finger on it, the road looked different than Trevor remembered, though not so different that he didn't recognize it in the dark. It was plenty dark, even with some moonlight and stars peeking through the canopy of trees. Only now did he realize how much he had actually missed those things.

Trevor still knew the route home. It would require miles of

walking, but it wasn't complicated. A straight shot for most of the way. Plus, he had more than enough energy. So he set out.

Odd-looking cars whizzed past, belching music Trevor didn't recognize. Some flashed their brights at him—as if to remind him to be careful—but none slowed to a stop. The vehicles seemed rounder than he was accustomed to, sleeker, with paint jobs so flawless he wondered if they were all brand-new. As he trudged on, they became fewer and far between, which told him he was entering the dead of night.

The air held a damp coolness, an omen of fall. It wasn't anywhere close to cold, but it was a pleasant reminder of how cooler weather can stiffen you up, put you on the path to alertness. Trevor's head, like his body, had spent so much time swimming. It was finally beginning to surface. He was coming to understand that this was not the world he had left.

His route didn't take him past stores, or commercial districts, but it did take him through the forest and past some fields that he remembered as farmland. Now those fields were occupied by small residential neighborhoods, spreading out like lava flows, their porch lights glowing orange in the hazy air.

Their presence was certainly disconcerting. As strange as his existence had been at the pool, this was supposed to be a return to normal. Yet he had no idea what normal was supposed to look like anymore. Or how to find it. His only choice seemed to be to keep walking and maybe the answer would reveal itself.

It must have taken a few hours to reach the neighborhood where he grew up, and by the time he got there, fatigue was setting in. It was still dark, but his eyes had adjusted. So had his mind. He had started to convince himself that all the things he was seeing hadn't changed. The problem was that he was misremembering them.

Arriving at his house highlighted a literal hole in that logic. Because there was one thing he couldn't have misremembered: a pool in his backyard. Unthinkable. He'd asked his parents countless times for a pool over the years, and they'd always laughed off the proposal. "Should we buy a Rolls-Royce too?" his father usually said in response.

Yet there was clearly a pool there now. Or was it a mirage? The clichéd image of a mirage always featured a man crawling through the desert, spotting a shimmering oasis on the horizon, and using every last bit of energy to surge toward it, desperate for a drink. In Trevor's case, he was ambling down a suburban road, spotting a dark and lustrous stretch of water, and then stopping at the edge of the grass to marvel at its very existence, desperate for . . . what exactly?

A swim. Obviously, a swim.

Entirely real. Entirely lovely. Late summer had treated the water well, and Trevor slipped into it like a second skin. It made him think of one of the many silly conversations they'd had early on at the natural pool. Schultz had mused that it would be fantastic if you were handed a printout of your statistics in the last moments of your life. Basic things like "hours slept," "TV reruns watched," or "french fries eaten."

As Trevor soaked, he wondered what percentage of his life he had already spent in the water. Was he inching toward marine mammal? Thoughts of the water led to thoughts of Sarah. How much time had Trevor spent with her? How many kisses had they shared? How long had he spent looking into her eyes, talking to her? He'd been avoiding dwelling on such memories, distracting himself, because he knew how painful the memories might be. And they could only lead to painful questions.

Was she out here somewhere too? Was she thinking about him? If he went to look for her, what would he say if he found her? What would *she* say?

The questions were too much to handle. They gave way to tears. It was the first time in a long time that Trevor had cried. He didn't wail. Didn't blubber. Still, he felt the grief cascade over him, unobstructed, and he knew this was necessary. So, he let it happen. Quietly. Alone.

Or so he thought.

"It'll be all right, buddy," said a voice. A man's voice. A familiar one.

At the other end of the pool, there was movement. A dark figure sitting up in a deck chair. It had been so long since Trevor had pool-hopped. His fight or flight instinct was rusty. Instead of bolting, he froze.

"Don't worry. I'm not calling the cops. Or even asking you to leave."

Shouldn't it be the other way around? This was Trevor's house. *He* should be the one doing the calling, the asking. This guy should be leaving. But Trevor couldn't manage to say anything other than, "Sorry."

"No apologies necessary," the voice replied. "I was young. I was even in your exact same predicament once. And a woman was kind and generous to me. So, I'm paying it forward."

"Okay," Trevor said softly. Something more than worry was settling in, something closer to terror. Because not only did this voice sound familiar. It sounded like . . . his own.

The area was too bathed in shadows and darkness for Trevor to see the man's face. He assumed the man couldn't see him as well. Still, Trevor had an idea of what the man might look like, and the idea made him shudder.

"Boy, oh boy, you're dredging up some memories," the man said.

"Yeah?" Trevor replied. "Like . . . good memories?"

"Sure. I mean . . ."

"What?"

"You're just making me think about a friend I haven't thought about in ages. A girl." The man stopped for a moment. "I don't know why I'm telling you this."

"Because . . . I don't know. Because I'm here? Because I'm listening?"

The man sighed. "Good a reason as any."

"So, what are your memories of her? The friend? The girl?"

"Nothing really, just teenage stuff," the man said. "Though I guess you'd relate. One summer the two of us tried to swim every pool in Sutton."

Terror. Yes terror. That was what Trevor was feeling, and yet he couldn't resist asking a question. "Did you swim them all?"

"All but one," the man said. "That woman I told you about. You know, the kind and generous one? She caught us swimming in her pool."

"You and the girl?"

"Yeah, and a few other friends. The lady got a real kick out of it, and she encouraged us to swim more. Told us about this hidden pool out in the woods. A natural pool. Everyone was raring to go, but I was exhausted. And a bit fed up. So I asked the girl to drive me home."

An alternate history flashed across Trevor's mind, a set of pages he hadn't yet explored in a Choose Your Own Adventure novel. Only this was his life. *His* life.

His voice quivered as he asked, "You skipped it?"

"You don't really want to hear all this. A story about me *not* doing something? Not exactly interesting."

"It is to me," Trevor said, and the man fell silent for a moment. Trevor wasn't sure if he was going to say anything else, so he asked again, his voice getting stronger because he needed to know. "You skipped it?"

It took another few moments, and then the man cleared his throat. Finally, he spoke in a soft but firm voice. "We skipped it. Over the next couple weeks, we swam the rest of the pools on our list, but never got around to that hidden one. Then off we went to college. And you know how those things go."

Trevor suspected he knew how those things went, but he wasn't exactly sure. He searched for a response. "I . . . I . . . I . . ."

"Are you still in high school?"

"No. I graduated at the . . . beginning of the summer."

"Oh, then you might know my daughter. She's a junior at Sutton."

"I . . . I'm actually . . ."

"Sorry," the man said. "You don't need to tell me anything about yourself. Not even your name. That's fine. I'll make a useless witness when the police show up."

They shared another moment of silence, broken only by the sound of the water as Trevor's body moved through it to a spot in the pool where the shadows were even thicker.

"That was a joke, by the way," the man said. "The police aren't coming. All I ask is that you don't be too loud. Everyone inside is asleep."

"Your family?" Trevor asked.

"Wife, two kids, dog," the man said. "A cliché, I know. At least the fence around the pool isn't picket, right? Obviously doesn't keep out intrepid pool-hoppers like yourself, though."

Indeed. Of the fences Trevor had encountered, this had been one of the easier ones to scale. It was almost as if the man was inviting trespassers.

"What do you do?" Trevor asked. "I mean, to afford all this?"

"You're not trying to steal my identity, are you?" the man said.

"No sir . . . I . . . I—"

"Kidding again," the man said. "I grew up in this house. Which helps. And I edit the *Journal*, which doesn't pay a ton, but it's enough."

"What happened to the girl?" Trevor asked. "She's not your wife, is she?"

This made the man laugh. Not a boisterous laugh, but not a sad one. A wistful one? And he said, "You're full of questions, aren't you?"

"Sorry."

"It's fine. It's . . . nothing ever happened with her. I think she married a guy named Kyle. Kevin? Something with a K. She's in Brooklyn. She writes. Essays and freelance stuff. Or at least that's what I remember from Instagram. I don't use it much anymore."

Trevor had no idea what Instagram was, and he didn't bother asking. There was a more pressing question. One he almost didn't want to know the answer to.

"The girl, what was her name?"

"Sarah," the man said. "Like half the girls I graduated with. Most were either Sarah or Jennifer or Katie or—"

"Heather?" Trevor asked.

"Yeah," the man said. "I knew a Heather."

Obviously, a Bev and a Lori too. There was no need to even ask him about those names, because there was no debating who the man was. Or more accurately, who the man had once been. The fact sent Trevor's heart racing.

The man must've heard Trevor breathing heavily, because

he asked, "Do you want me to leave you alone? I'm here talking your ear off when you're obviously dealing with something difficult."

Trevor splashed a little water on his face to collect himself. Closed his eyes. "I'm okay," he said. "A little overwhelmed. Thinking about . . . someone."

"If it's about a girl. Or guy. Or, I don't know, someone you . . . Oh, forget it. I'm getting too personal."

"No. You can say it. I want you to say it."

"It's nothing. It's just . . . feelings pass."

The man said it without enough conviction. The pauses were dead giveaways. Trevor knew that better than anyone.

"Do you still think about her?" Trevor asked. "Sarah, I mean?"

There was another pause and then the man said, "No. Not much. She's a great girl . . . woman, I mean. But it wasn't the right fit. For either of us. I found the right fit for my life. I hope she found hers."

The right fit included the house that Trevor grew up in. He could only assume what that meant about his parents. This was a case where he didn't want to ask.

"So, you don't have any—" Trevor started to say.

And the man finished the sentence, his voice sounding so similar to Trevor's that it might as well have been one person speaking. "Regrets?" he said. "I've had a few. But then again, too few to mention."

Sinatra. Trevor got the reference. But he didn't respond.

So the man said, "That one is probably before your time.

But it bears repeating. Always more wisdom in song lyrics than you might realize."

"Yeah," Trevor said because that's all he needed to say. He knew exactly what the man meant.

"Thing is this, though," the man went on. "If you're gonna start regretting choices, then you better start working to change the part of yourself that made those choices. Then you'll see those regrets turn into something else. They'll become an essential part of who you are."

The words felt familiar, and that's when Trevor realized that they reminded him of a poem. English class, junior year. Robert Frost. "The Road Not Taken." The class discussed its themes. Choice versus fate. Individualism. Regrets. In the end, everyone in the class seemed to be on the same page. That if life presents you with a fork in the road, you must take the "road less traveled by," or else you'll regret it.

Now Trevor wasn't so sure. This man seemed happy, right? Content, at least. And he didn't take the road less traveled by, did he? He simply learned from his mistakes.

Or maybe it was all an act. Maybe he was trying to justify his mistakes, because the missed opportunity of having a more interesting life was too difficult to face. Trevor couldn't ask him if this was what he was doing, of course. So, he asked something else instead.

"Do you ever regret buying a pool?"

The man chuckled. "Oh, they're not cheap, I'll tell you that. But no. Don't regret that for a second."

"I always wanted one when I was a kid," Trevor said.

"Me too, buddy, me too," the man said softly, and he took a deep breath. "You know, you're an easy guy to talk to. Too easy. Before I know it, I'm gonna be giving you all my passwords."

"I can leave," Trevor told him.

"No," the man said. "Enjoy the water for as long as you want. I suspect you need the time."

"For what?"

"To take a breath. Before whatever you got going on next. College. Work. An illustrious career as an influencer. The standard."

"Oh. Okay."

"Congrats on graduating and good luck to you. As for me, I'm heading off to bed," the man said, and then he rose from the chair at the other side of the pool.

"Thank you, sir," Trevor replied, which felt like the most insignificant thing he could possibly say, given the situation.

"Return the favor someday," the man replied, and he headed back to the house.

It was the house that Trevor had lived in for his entire life. But Trevor didn't live here anymore, did he? Not since he stepped out of Sarah's car, walked down that trail, swam at that—

Was the natural pool his true home now? Could he go back? Was that what he needed?

No. That place wasn't meant for him anymore. It was meant for that girl in the white jean shorts, and her friends, and whoever else was lucky (or unlucky) enough to find it.

As the man opened the back door, Trevor had the urge to follow him, to scurry up the stairs and burrow under the covers in his bed, to sleep for the rest of the night and wake to discover it was all a dream. But the urge disappeared as soon as the man stepped inside and closed the door.

He took a long and deep breath.

She comes out onto the stoop and sits down on a step. Saying she looks gorgeous seems conceited. But, come on, she does look good. Or should I say that I look good? Because I can see that clearly now. She is me.

Yes. *She* is *me*. I'm looking at myself. About twenty years older. Longer hair. Tighter clothes, which I guess are in fashion now? They fit well, in any case. Plus, I have a tattoo on my forearm. How 'bout that?

Over on the stoop, I'm also holding a mug, which steams in the summer air. Means we're probably both drinking coffee. Or perhaps I'm drinking herbal tea. It's well past dinner. Even a Coke after dinner makes me fidgety. Though maybe I've gotten used tó caffeine. A long time has passed.

It should be strange to watch myself. It should be terrifying. But it's not. It's oddly comforting. And as I watch myself, I find I'm mirroring myself. Over on the stoop, I look left, look right, adjust my hair, take a sip. Then I do all those same things over here at the café.

From this distance, I doubt I'd notice me, spying over a coffee mug, but I don't think it even matters because I hardly turn my head in this direction. More interesting things to look at obviously. I watch me sip my drink as the world drifts by. It's peaceful.

I also watch as I say hi to neighbors. As I pet a dog who comes to sniff my flip-flops. And I watch as I finish the drink and set the mug on the step next to me. I watch me sit there for a long time, until I rise from the stoop and amble back inside.

Okay. I'm okay. It's gonna be okay.

Wait. No.

How about better than okay? Fantastic even? Yes. That's what it is. That's what I'll be. And this is exactly what I came to see. I can't begin to describe how satisfying it is.

I get up from my seat at the café and I go for a walk. West, toward Manhattan and the water. I don't belong here. That's clear to me. It's not just that I've missed out on so much. It's that . . .

How can I exist here if I already exist here? Do I even want to?

The only thing I can think to do right now is the only thing I know how to do anymore. I keep walking until I reach a slender park that kisses the river. The East River, not far from where it meets up with the Hudson, just like on the map.

People jog and bike along a path. Walk their adorable dogs. Swim in the water too? Definitely not. The river is probably polluted. But what do I care?

I don't. The fence isn't very high. I've climbed way higher. I suppose I could get in trouble for this, so I wait until no one is looking. Then I hop over in a single, smooth jump.

I stand here for a moment, gazing across the water at the hazy and pulsing city. I made it here. I'm *making* it here. Exactly like I hoped I would. It feels incredible.

But what about you?

I don't know what you'll find when you finally make it back. Yourself, probably. I know because I found you. So easily. First in the masthead of the *Sutton Journal.* Then on that computer in the library. Property records, wedding announcement, the whole shebang. Trevor Cleary, back home, trading his *I love you*s with someone else, editing the weekly paper with its police blotter and high school sports. I do hope it's the "good life" you told me about. I desperately want it to make you feel the way I feel right now. You deserve happiness.

And I'm sorry. Not for leaving, but for thinking your happiness was any less significant because it wasn't my happiness. I was never angry at you. Only at myself. For being scared about what came after the pool. I guess we were all like that. Maybe I still am. Though not as much as before.

The sun is low, and the sky is taking on a reddish hue. On the river, a sailboat courses by. People on board sip wine and beer and listen to music. Purple lights line the edges of the hull, and their reflections wriggle alongside the boat like a school of tropical fish. As I look down at the water, there's something fizzing in my body. I reach my hands out to dive, but as I do, my hands dissolve into the air. Disappear like mist in the wind.

Then my arms too.

I close my eyes, and I relive our singular and spectacular adventure. I bask in what we had until it's imprinted on my soul.

I'm ready to start over. I'm . . .

night swimming

Even though the air was cool and thick with moisture, Trevor's clothes were dry. The magic of summer. There was a haze upon the horizon, an indication of dawn. Walking south, away from the house, Trevor had no plan.

That was okay for now. He wasn't hungry. He was no longer tired. He had grown accustomed to living alone, so more alone time couldn't hurt him. Eventually, he'd need a permanent place to settle down, but he wasn't too worried now. His main worry was, to put it bluntly, his face. People would recognize him, wouldn't they? He was still trying to get his head around the passage of time and what his presence in this version of the world meant, but he was quite certain he might run into an old friend or acquaintance. And then what?

Explanations were impossible, but perhaps there was someone out there who could offer some guidance. The person who guided them in the first place. It would mean more walking, but Trevor was up for it. To avoid any potential meetings, he chose to take a longer route through quiet neighborhoods and semirural roads. Or what he knew to be semirural roads. As he'd already discovered, such things are never static.

* * *

The sun had climbed halfway up the sky when he arrived at the purple house. It was painted blue now. The pool remained in the back, placid and sparkling in the late morning light, but there were no purple decorations surrounding it. The house looked, for lack of a better word, normal.

Was Trevor's memory faulty? Was this place ever purple?

Of course it was. The blue paint was peeling in spots, and Trevor could see hints of purple underneath, whispers of its previous life. He could speculate on whether the Purple Lady had passed away or found another home, but the indication was clear. She no longer lived here. Probably hadn't for some time. No surprise, though he was still disappointed. He didn't have anyone else to reach out to. Except the others.

Lori. Schultz. Heather. Jared. Bev. Buck. Sarah.

Did two versions of them exist in this world as well? For some reason, Trevor didn't think it was possible. Because he was starting to think the same thing about himself. How could there be two of him? Surely one was an imposter, a dream, a phantom of a life that could've never happened. When the others returned home, they must've felt the same way. So what did they do? Did they seek one another out for explanations?

Surely, Sarah didn't. When she took off, she undoubtedly left the pool, and everyone else, behind her. So where did she go? Did she figure out there was an older version of herself here? Did she try to find that person? Perhaps in New York

City? Trevor took a moment to imagine how that might play out. Different than his meeting with himself, but also the same. Terrifying at first, but ultimately necessary. It made him happy for her. To know she had a chance to peel back the veil on her future was extremely comforting. He still had feelings for her, but no ill will. It was possible that he might never see her again. His heart could deal with that. At least for the moment. His only true desire was to walk, to wander. So that's what he did.

He pressed on, down the loneliest roads he could find. Before long, it became obvious that this era in his life was truly over. He'd essentially known that when he left the pool, but now, having seen what his life might become, he accepted it. His body fizzed and sparkled, carbonated by a belief. This future, this *now*, it was waiting for him if he wanted it. Did he want it, though?

No. Not even a little bit of it. That feeling could change, obviously, but at the moment all he wanted was some faith, an unwavering belief that there was more than one future waiting for him. Actually, it was more than just a want. That belief was an absolute necessity. It was the only way he could let go and start over. The forever night was real, more real than anything he'd ever experienced. It had also served its purpose. Trevor marched on through the late summer morning.

Whether it was a conscious decision or not was debatable, but he soon found himself approaching a place he'd never been before. It wasn't far from the natural pool, and while not quite as hidden, it didn't reveal itself until he was right upon it. Off the road, past a field where a graffiti-stained water tower once stood, through the brambles and brush, Trevor pushed his way out onto the cliffside at the edge of Hupper Hill.

It was not as he'd imagined. It was a lovely spot, without a doubt. But instead of making Sutton look impressive, it made the town look flat and unremarkable. The streets, the fields, the houses, the pools, they were all there. They just didn't fill him with the awe that he had hoped they would. They did, however, spark a memory.

Sarah's paper airplane. Her plan had been to launch the map from here and let it swoop over their dominion. At the time, when she described it to him, it seemed impossibly romantic. Now it made Trevor smile at how silly it was. Though silly in the right way. Silly in the way that people should be silly.

Even though he was smiling, a tear slipped down Trevor's face. He was scared. So very terrified. Which was natural and, in a way, reassuring. It meant he was feeling what he was supposed to be feeling. Unsure of himself and the world. Deep down, he didn't know whether things would be okay for him. But he was fairly certain that there was a space for him out there. In some place, at some time. Just not here, not now.

Trevor closed his eyes. He sat down in the grass. Bee balm, with its fragrant lilac-colored blooms, brushed against his face. There were no people, or even cars, within earshot. He was entirely alone. He didn't have to tell himself that this was it. His bones, his blood, his everything . . . it already knew. It was time to try again.

He lay back and put his arms out wide. Breathing deep, his

lungs were bottomless. As they pulled in the air, they became the air. So too did the rest of his body, slowly vaporizing in the ripe morning. His mind, however, held on for a moment longer. He swam backward through memories of the night, absorbing their feeling if not their meaning—like a song whose lyrics he wouldn't remember but whose melody he would always be able to hum—until finally, finally, he reached deep into his past and grabbed ahold of a solid edge.

Acknowledgments

I'm not sure when I first sat down to write *Night Swimming*, but the idea for this story has been germinating in my mind for decades. Perhaps since the end of my senior year of high school, when my friends and I headed down to the local art-house, Manlius Cinema, to watch a movie called *Dazed and Confused*. We certainly weren't the biggest partiers at our school, but the film's celebratory spirit was infectious and inspirational. Could we have a summer even half as revelatory as the night depicted in Richard Linklater's coming-of-age tale? We were determined to try. So began a long and lazy season of adventures and bonding, with mix tapes providing the soundtrack. While we didn't set out on a mission like Trevor and Sarah, there may have even been a few spontaneous and surreptitious incidents of night swimming.

I want to thank all my friends from Fayetteville Manlius High School who made that summer so memorable. I tip my hat to Richard Linklater for creating that transformative masterpiece, and so many other masterpieces. Michael Stipe and R.E.M. wrote the song that inspired the title and themes of this novel, and while I don't make mix tapes anymore, there will always be room for "Nightswimming" on my playlists. For the distinct turn in the story, I owe a debt of gratitude to the work of two very different artists who share some very similar narrative devices: Stephen King and Luis Buñuel. Not every teen's idea of a dynamic duo, but hey, I'm old.

My tireless agent, Michael Bourret, was the first person to see potential in the opening pages of my strange little story, and I'm so fortunate that he convinced me to write the entire thing. My ever-perceptive editors Alex Wolfe and Rob Valois encouraged me to expand and deepen what was once too slim and slippery to work as a novel. Much of the mystery and emotion you find in these pages is because of their illuminating notes. Kudos. Publisher Francisco Sedita has been a constant supporter of my writing, and I'm proud to say that this is my sixth book with Penguin Workshop. If you love how this novel looks as much as I do, you can thank Dana Lédl for creating the spectacular cover art, Mary Claire Cruz for leading the innovative design, and compositor Kelly Kingsbury from Six Red Marbles for making sure everything was in its right place. Copyeditor Ana Deboo and proofreaders Rima Weinberg and Danielle Colburn kept me honest and provided well-needed lessons in grammar and logic. Meanwhile, publicist Aubrey Clemans has been out there making sure you know this book exists, and it appears she has succeeded.

Finally, I want to thank my family, particularly my wife, Cate, and my children, Hannah and Rowan, who are constantly showing me that I've chosen my best path in life, and who will always stop what they're doing to jump in the water with me.